By Miko Martin

MARCO AND THE TIGER

WEEKLY READER
CHILDREN'S BOOK CLUB

MARCO AND

Illustrated by

LORENCE F. BJORKLUND

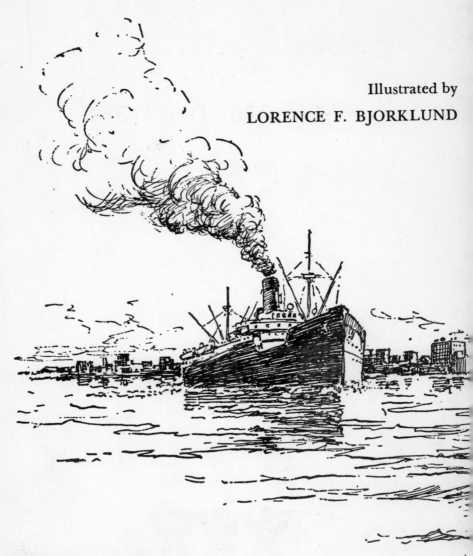

**Presented by
Weekly Reader
Children's Book Club**

THE TIGER

by John Foster

DODD, MEAD & COMPANY
New York

The characters and situations in this book are wholly fictional and imaginative: they do not portray and are not intended to portray any actual persons or parties.

Library of Congress Catalog Card Number: AC 67-10438
Printed in the United States of America
Weekly Reader Book Club Edition

To Miss Beeden

CONTENTS

1. In the Courtyard √   9
2. Tiger Tricks   19
3. Marco's Father   25
4. Marco Puts It in Writing   33
5. Tiger Talk   41
6. Man-to-Man Talk   50
7. Mrs. Drack Has a Surprise   59
8. Here Comes the Parade!   63
9. Things Are Not as They Seem   74
10. Ham on Rye   88
11. Under the Bed Sheet   97
12. The Fight   107
13. The Boy from Niger   111
14. A Walk through the Park   124

1

IN THE COURTYARD

Marco stood on the sidewalk in front of 420 Royal Street, in New Orleans, gazing up at the door a moment or two before knocking. It was quite a door. It was the kind of door you didn't mess with. It was huge and black, with big square iron nails and heavy iron hinges shaped like spearheads.

Marco took a deep breath. Then he reached up and banged the iron knocker, which was shaped like a fist.

"Paper boy!" he called.

No answer. But from somewhere far beyond the door came what sounded like a man, a large man, clearing his throat without much hope of success.

It was about four o'clock on a hot Thursday afternoon in March. And if you think New Orleans can't get hot in March, then you have never been in New Orleans during the month of March. It seemed pretty much like any other afternoon around that time of year. Of course, Marco, who was eleven, had no way of knowing that it would be an afternoon he would remember all his life.

Behind him, on Royal Street, a steady stream of cars went swishing past. Marco paid no attention. Nuts to them! He wasn't studying cars.

He took another whack at the knocker.

"I say again," he called, "it's Marco—Marco Fennerty, Junior, to be exact, collecting for the *States-Item*."

Then, glancing at his route book he yelled, "Hey, Perry!"

The owner of the house at 420 Royal, according to the route book, was Perry, O. K. Mr. Perry's full name was Oscar Kermet Perry. But Marco had it in his head that the man's first name was Perry and that he was one guy who was okay. Marco had been on the route only a month and this was his first day collecting, so there was a lot he had to learn. And he had never seen Mr. Perry.

Again no one answered Marco's call. But again that sound came from somewhere deep behind the door.

"If that *is* you, Perry, and you *are* clearing your throat," Marco said, "you don't seem to be getting anywhere, do you?"

He's probably got a cold, poor fella, Marco thought. But I *do* wish he would open up.

Marco squared his shoulders. He parked his bicycle and snapped the padlock on the rear wheel. Then he marched back to the door as though he carried a tomahawk instead of just his route book.

He was not a large boy. He was, in fact, rather small—if you didn't count his eyes and ears. But he was so quick and so fierce in combat that the bigger boys left him alone as a rule. Marco liked to think to himself that he carried TNT in both fists.

He was, as he also liked to think to himself, a boy without fear.

He gazed at the door and the hinges that were shaped like spearheads and at the knocker that was shaped like a fist. Then he looked at the doorknob, which was shaped like a doorknob.

He called out once more, giving briefly his name, occupation, and reason for being here. Then, taking hold of the doorknob, he gave it a turn, calling, "Perry, can I collect, please?"

There was a soft click.

Then, slowly and silently, the great black door opened wide. Marco leaped inside and the door shut behind him. He found himself in a carriageway that was like a long, dark tunnel. At the end of it was a large courtyard, lighted up by the afternoon sun.

In the French Quarter of New Orleans, there are courtyards, and there are courtyards. Marco had been around enough to know that this was not one of the best. Yet it had something. Yes, it did. It certainly did. His breath went out in a long, soft sigh.

"Gungah!" Marco said. It was an expression that made no sense whatever, but it was all his own.

The courtyard reminded him of a garden—a lost and forgotten garden. Maybe, he thought, it's just seeing it this way, all bright and green at the end of the dark tunnel. It was like something seen through the wrong end of a telescope.

But there was something about this place that he felt more than he saw. What it was, he didn't know. But it had something to do with his heart beating so fast and the sudden dryness in his mouth. Somewhere ahead he could hear a fountain splashing busily to itself as he started down the musty carriageway, tiptoeing on the flagstones.

Why are you tiptoeing? he asked himself. You, a boy without fear (who carries TNT in both fists)? He had no answer to that one, but, for some reason or other, he could not stop walking on the tips of his toes.

He kept calling to Perry, but Mr. Perry didn't answer....

Finally, Marco stepped out into the courtyard, blinking in the soft yellow light, and glanced around wide-eyed. He shook his shaggy blond head.

It's a pity, he said to himself, the way some people will let these fine old houses go to rack and ruin.

The courtyard had been pretty much left to itself for

some time, maybe years. The big stone fountain in one corner was covered with black, evil-looking mold. A thick clump of bamboo was growing every which way in the opposite corner. In the center of the courtyard, a huge concrete flowerpot had split open (maybe from last winter's freeze) and the big green plant growing there was half in, half out of the pot.

To the left, a rickety wooden staircase climbed, staggering, up to a second-floor balcony that went around three sides of the courtyard. Gazing up there, Marco saw broken black windows, like blind eyes, behind a railing with half its spokes kicked out.

On the fourth side of the courtyard was a high brick wall that seemed to be laced together with vines. It was topped with pieces of colored glass that glinted and glowed in the dying sunlight.

There was, or seemed to be, a curious hush in the patio. The sounds of the street—the roaring and snorting of buses, the impatient honking of horns as people rushed home from work—seemed to be echoing from far, far away.

Then again there came the strange noise Marco had heard before. It was coming from one of the two big wooden doors on the uptown side of the courtyard, where carriages had been kept in the old days.

The door on the left?

Or the one on the right?

Squaring his shoulders, Marco went to the door on the left. He knocked, then lifted the rusty iron latch.

For some time afterward, because he was a boy who thought about such matters, Marco wondered if all the things that started to happen to him then would ever have happened if he had opened the other door.

"Perry?" he said. "It's Marco the paper boy . . ."

His voice, which wasn't much at this point anyhow, died

off completely. It was even darker inside the doorway than the carriageway had been. Then Marco became aware of two large yellow eyes gazing steadily out at his large—but not all *that* large—brown eyes.

"Perry," he asked, "are you taking anything for that cold?"

Then, slowly and without making a fuss about it, a huge Royal Bengal tiger came padding out of the darkness into the courtyard.

Marco squared his shoulders, rubbed the route book against his snub nose, and said in a husky voice, "Hello, Tiger."

The tiger gave a long, soft growl, as if trying to clear his throat, or as if maybe just thinking of something else, and started toward Marco.

He put his mighty paws down with great care, as though not sure the flagstones would hold his weight. He walked as if saying to himself, "I'm gonna show every muscle in my body and, brother, I got a million of 'em." As he came slouching toward Marco, he kept wagging his head from side to side, making tiger faces and giving short, quiet tiger growls that sounded like, "Ho!" and "Ha!" and "Ah!" and "Hah!"

Marco was a boy without fear but he wasn't stupid.

He went up the wall like a monkey, clutching the vines hand over hand. Then he eased himself down on the top. The broken glass was worn down like old teeth and didn't hurt too much.

Marco and the tiger looked at each other a good long time.

"You're a handsome animal, Tiger," Marco said at last.

The tiger opened his great red jaws wide, wide, wide, and yawned. *"Um-ow-w-w-uhn-n-n-UGH!"*

It was, by far, the finest yawn Marco had ever seen. But,

clearly, the tiger was telling him that flattery would get him nowhere. Yet Marco had felt that he must say *something*. The silence had become embarrassing.

What he had said was nothing but the truth, though. The tiger was more than ten feet long from the tip of his black nose to the black tuft on the end of his tail. He would have weighed more than four hundred pounds with a full stomach (which it wasn't). He was reddish orange, with neat black stripes. He had a fine, big head, and the hair on his cheeks was long and white, like a well-kept beard.

Yes, there was no arguing the point. He was a handsome animal.

He gazed up at Marco in an interested manner, switching his tail back and forth. (It *was* switching, Marco noticed. Not wagging.) His teeth were worn down like the glass on the wall, but they looked as though they could hurt plenty if he wanted them to.

Marco knew, of course, that the tiger was not the Perry, O. K., listed in his route book. Probably, Marco thought, good ol' Perry kept him as a watch tiger or a pet.

Then Marco noticed something else. The tiger was carrying his right front paw in the air.

Aw, Marco thought, he's got a thorn in his foot, poor fella. If I take it out, I'll have me a friend for life, like that guy Androcles and the lion in *Aesop's Fables.*

But how long would that life last if he tried to get buddy-buddy with a tiger?

Angrily, Marco put the coward thought out of his mind. I can handle this, he told himself. I *will* handle it. I'm eleven.

Slowly, he climbed down the wall. He kept watching the tiger over his shoulder, ready to scurry right back up again if it seemed a good idea.

Watch the ears, he told himself. Watch those ears, boy.

Marco and the tiger looked at each other a good long time. "You're a handsome animal, Tiger," Marco said at last.

If they go back, you go up—fast—because he's going to spring.

Coming down, Marco had some bad moments, for the ears would twitch, twitch, twitch. And every time Marco jumped, jumped, jumped. But then he decided that the twitching was just a nervous habit, which it was, and down he came with a thump.

He had never stopped talking on the way.

"Oh, now, look here, Tiger," he said. "I see by the way you're holding your right front paw in the air that you have picked up a thorn. I'll just take it out—or the piece of glass, as the case may be—and you and I will be lifelong friends."

"Ho! Ha! Ah! Hah!"

Patiently, the tiger waited as Marco, still talking, walked up to him. The boy knew he wasn't making a lot of sense. But he thought that, right now, the meaning of the words was less important than the sound of them. He tried, still talking, to think of words with soft sounds—words with plenty of *s's* and *m's* and *w's*.

"Yes, sir," Marco said. "Yes, siree. Just you wait a second or so and I'll bring you instant relief. By the way, I'm Marco Fennerty, Junior. I just made eleven. I'm the son of Sergeant Marco Fennerty of the New Orleans Police Department— only son and only child, I might add—so please keep that in mind, Tiger."

Easily, the tiger sat down.

"Ho!" he growled. "Ha! Ah! Hah!"

Gently, ever so gently, Marco took hold of his huge paw. Talking, talking about this, that, and the other, he turned the paw up and felt the rough black pad. Then he ran his fingers through the tufts of silky-soft black fur between the toes. He couldn't find a thing.

He pressed the pad, and the tiger's mighty claws slipped

out like four ivory daggers. They were awful weapons indeed.

"Ah!" Marco said.

"Ho! Ha!" said the tiger.

Marco felt just the least bit silly. This was actually the
first time in his life that he had held the paw of a tiger. But
the main thing about the matter was that there was no thorn
in the paw.

No glass either.

Nothing.

Marco still held the paw while he tried to decide what in the world to do with it. After all, he thought, as silly as he felt now, he would feel a whole lot sillier if he just let go and walked away after making such a big deal about it to begin with.

Then he had an idea.

2

TIGER TRICKS

"Shake hands, Tiger," Marco said.

He took the big, heavy paw in both his hands and pumped it up and down. It was somewhat like working out with a furry bar bell.

"You do that very well," he said. "I don't suppose you know any other tricks."

The tiger studied Marco with his great yellow eyes as if, hard as he tried, he couldn't quite figure this kid out. Marco was used to seeing such an expression on people when they looked at him, but the tiger had a way all his own. It was unsettling, to say the least.

For a moment Marco gazed deep into the tiger's eyes. Then he glanced away, rubbing his nose with the route book. For that moment it had seemed to the boy that he could see in the tiger's eyes the jungle, with all its wildness and awful power and raw beauty and its spookiness.

There was something else about those eyes. What was it? Marco could not decide.

"I'll bet you escaped from the circus, Tiger," he said. "And in the circus tigers learn all the latest tricks."

Stepping back, he pointed one finger at the tiger.

"Roll over!"

The tiger made no move, no sound. But from the look on his face, he seemd to be saying, "Eh?"

Marco raised the finger and brought it down again.

"Play dead, Tiger!"

Watching Marco with polite interest, the tiger slowly lowered his right front paw to the ground. Then, slowly, he lifted his left front paw.

If only I had a whip, Marco thought. A whip to crack and a gun to fire in the air like the animal trainers in the circus have. Then, boy, I could make him jump through flaming hoops and everything.

"Come on, Tiger," he said, "I'm afraid we're not making our best effort. Now if you'll give me your attention, I'll try to show you what I mean. For my first trick I'll play dead. . . ."

Marco threw himself on the ground, then rolled over on his back with his hands and feet in the air. He gave the tiger an encouraging smile. "See? It's easy."

For maybe thirty seconds the tiger gazed at Marco lying there. Then he came up behind Marco and stared down at him for maybe another twenty seconds. Marco had to roll his head back to see the tiger. It is one thing to look into a tiger's solemn striped face. To look into a tiger's solemn striped face upside down is something else again—and hard on the neck muscles. But Marco did it.

Then the tiger took his left front paw, the one that was hanging in the air anyway, and gave Marco a swipe with it.

The courtyard, as noted, was large. Marco went rolling over and over and over and over until he bumped into the fountain in the corner. "Hey!"

Before he could get up, the tiger had padded over to him. Then, with another swipe of his paw, he sent Marco rolling over and over and over and over to the other side of the courtyard, where he went crashing and banging into the bamboo.

Marco jumped to his feet.

"Don't mess with me, Tiger!" he yelled. "I may appear small to you, but I am quick and I carry TNT in both fists!"

The tiger raised one furry white eyebrow. His feelings were hurt.

Marco, however, was feeling hurt all over. In his travels back and forth across the patio, he had scraped elbows and knees and had received minor damage to wrists, ankles, and nose. But his main problem was dizziness. You might think that rolling one way makes you dizzy, and rolling the other undizzies you. It doesn't.

Gungah!

He kept wobbling around in a very silly manner, like a top coming to the end of its spin. To keep from falling flat on his face, he grabbed a thick stalk of bamboo. Besides being dizzy, he was plenty mad. The tiger kept swimming past in a red haze.

Then Marco thought of school tomorrow.

"Hey, Marco, what happened to you?" the kids would say.

"Hmm?" he would ask.

"Where'd you get all the bobos?"

"Oh, *those*."

"Yeah, those. How'd yuh get 'em, hey?"

"Romping with my tiger."

"Your tiger!"

"He doesn't mean to be rough but"—and here he would give a shrug and a smile—"you know tigers."

Anger passed, then dizziness. When the tiger and the world were standing still again, Marco let go of the bamboo.

"Now, look here, Tiger," he said. "You're the one that's supposed to do the tricks—not me."

The tiger raised both furry eyebrows, as if to say, "Oh, really now?"

Then Marco had a thought.

"Well, after all, Tiger," he pointed out. "why should you do tricks, anyhow? You don't have to entertain me like that just because I'm your guest. We can have our romps and talks and all, but there will be no tricks. Agreed?"

The tiger smiled—or seemed to smile.

"I think we're going to be fine friends," Marco said. "But, really and truly, Tiger, you'll have to watch the rough stuff, you know? I bruise easily."

The tiger seemed sorry.

"And now it's getting late and I must go," Marco said. "Don't bother to see me to the door."

Then it occurred to him that he had better leave things

as he had found them, the main thing being the tiger. Marco opened the door of the animal's quarters and got ready for an argument. But the tiger seemed glad to go back inside.

"Good-by, Tiger," the boy said. "See you tomorrow."

From behind the door came what had first sounded to him like a man trying to clear his throat.

Marco went across the courtyard, now quite dark, and through the very dark carriageway. He let himself out, closing the heavy front door behind him. The Desire Street bus, all lighted up, roared past, then stopped at the corner with a hiss of air brakes. Cars went by, honking.

Slowly, deep in thought, Marco walked over to his bicycle and started to slip the key into the padlock. It was hard to believe, out here on the flashing, noisy street, filled with the fumes of burned gasoline, that what had happened in the courtyard had really happened.

Suddenly, he turned around and went back to the door with the hinges shaped like spearheads and the knocker shaped like a fist and the doorknob shaped like a doorknob. Then, not taking any chances, he whispered, "Please," and turned the knob.

The door swung open silently and easily. Marco went through the dark carriageway and across the courtyard to the two big wooden doors. Everything seemed to be in order. He squared his shoulders, humming a little tune he had just made up. Then he lifted the latch of the door on the left.

"Tiger?"

Close to the ground, two yellow fires burned in the darkness. The tiger was lying down. The fires went out, then came back on again as he blinked his eyes. He was rather surprised to see his funny little friend again so soon and, if the truth were known, not too happy about it. The afternoon had been great but tiring.

With a grunt or so and a couple of groans and a creak and a pop of his bones, he started to get to his feet.

"Please," Marco said, "don't get up. I just wanted to be sure that you were really there. I was afraid that I had just imagined you, if you follow me, Tiger. I am said to have a vivid imagination."

Well, there was no question about it. The tiger most certainly was there. Marco watched the two yellow fires that went out and came back on and then went out again, like blinker lights. Dot, dot, dash, dot . . .

He closed the door gently.

"Good night, Tiger," he whispered. "Sleep well."

The tiger gave a happy groan.

3

MARCO'S FATHER

Back on the street, Marco unlocked his bicycle and started to pedal home past the old brick buildings with their iron balconies lined with flowerpots. Royal was one way, going uptown. Far ahead of him were the glare and blare of Canal Street, all dressed up in its Carnival decorations.

With Mardi Gras coming next Tuesday, everyone was gayer and louder than usual. In the bright little apartments above the dark little shops on Royal, the boy could hear laughter and the sound of record music as the young couples living there prepared themselves for supper.

He made a right turn and rode over a block. Bourbon Street was agleam with neon signs and loud with the sounds of the jazz bands tuning up for the evening. He pedaled by a man in a white coat and cap who pushed a long white cart, chanting, "Oh, I got hot dogs, hot dogs, get 'em while they're hot!"

Marco wanted to chant back, "Oh, I know a tiger, tiger, and he knows me . . ." or something of the sort. He didn't, though. Then he heard a high, sharp whistle and, standing on the corner of Bourbon and Toulouse, he saw the Chief. He was a fine, tall man with a back as long and straight as the white cane he held. He carried the white cane (with the red tip) because he was blind. He had a slim silver whistle that he would blow whenever he wanted someone to help him across the street.

Marco was too polite to ask, but he was sure that the man had been a chief bosun's mate who had lost his eyesight when the USS *Bonhomme Richard* had defeated the HMS *Serapis* or in some other great American naval victory.

Marco enjoyed helping the Chief across the street. He always felt like an admiral, or at least the President of the United States, being piped aboard a warship.

"Hello, Chief," he said, jumping off his bike.

"Well, dog my cats, it's Marco," the Chief said.

This had always struck Marco as about the craziest thing a person could say, but he had never mentioned it. He liked the Chief, and the Chief liked him.

"What are you doing out so late, Marco?" the Chief asked.

"I'm glad you asked that question, Chief," Marco replied. "I was having a romp with my tiger."

"Well, dog my cats!" the Chief said again.

He blew another blast on his whistle for Marco's sake. Then he gave the boy his big, hard arm—an arm Marco was sure was covered with the finest quality tattoos. They started across the street, the Chief rolling along as if on the deck of a destroyer bucking heavy seas.

"Well, now, he really isn't *my* tiger," Marco admitted.

"I see," the blind man said.

"But he really is a tiger, and I really was having a romp with him."

"I see."

"Really!" Marco persisted.

"Well, dog my cats!"

Marco gazed up into the Chief's face in the light of the street lamp. His eyelids were closed down like windowshades

on his high, bronze cheekbones. He looked as though he were walking in his sleep.

"You don't believe I was having a romp with a tiger, do you?" Marco asked. "Do you, Chief?"

"Of course I do, Marco. Of course I do."

Of course he didn't.

The boy squared his shoulders. Adults didn't take him too seriously. But that went both ways.

"Thank you, Marco," the Chief said when they had reached his door. "Will you come up for a cup of jamoke?"

"Not tonight, thanks," Marco said, hopping on his bike. It was a regular joke between them. And it was one more reason why Marco thought the blind man had been a chief bosun's mate. Those guys were always drinking jamoke—whatever that was. He really liked the Chief.

When Marco reached home he wheeled his bicycle into the hallway and locked it. Then, carrying a paper, he ran up the three flights of creaky wooden stairs to his apartment. The building was old, old. The stairs were worn down by generations of other Marcos who, the boy liked to think, had gone on to become All-American quarterbacks, warriors, captains of industry, and policemen.

Marco's mother died when he was four. Since then, Sergeant Fennerty had hired one housekeeper after another to take care of his son while the sergeant was at the police station—which was most of the time. Sergeant Fennerty worked the night shift and sometimes the day shift and usually on Sunday because the younger policemen were always asking him to take their place so they could go fishing. Marco's father was too kindhearted to refuse.

Sergeant Fennerty was a small, gray-haired man with a twinkle in his eyes. He also had a .45-caliber bullet in his left leg, received in the line of duty. It was not, as Marco had to explain to his friends all the time, that his father particularly *liked* the bullet. The doctors just couldn't remove it. It made Marco's father limp a little—not a lot, just a little.

Marco was puffing pretty hard when he reached the top of the stairs. Opening the apartment door, he called, "Mrs. Drack, I'm home!"

Mrs. Drack was the latest housekeeper. She had come five weeks ago. Marco waited for her voice, which reminded him of two rusty razor blades rubbing together, to say, "So what?"

"Ahoy, Mrs. Drack!" he called. "The good ship Marco is home!"

But Mrs. Drack wasn't. She often wasn't when the boy reached home. She loved to walk along Canal Street, looking in the store windows, or to stroll through the city's graveyards, looking at the tombs. Then lots of times she would take in a movie or go to some friend's house for a little poker, so that her charge would be asleep when she finally came home.

Marco wandered through the lonesome apartment, humming another tune he had just made up. At the front window he stopped to gaze across the rooftops at the sharp steeples of St. Louis Cathedral, three black spikes against the dark blue sky.

A freighter, lit up like a Christmas tree, was sweeping around the broad black curve of the Mississippi River, headed for the open sea. She gave a long blast on her horn, which the Cathedral pigeons found most annoying. The river was high and swift from the spring thaw in the north, and Marco could see plenty of driftwood rushing past.

Mighty, mighty Mississippi, he thought. It must have been fun in the old days when the river smashed through the levees and flooded the city—everyone paddling around in boats. Gungah!

He studied his nose in the bathroom mirror. Yessir. It was good and skinned. He painted it and his other wounds with iodine. There were other, gentler things in the medicine cabinet, but Marco just thought the occasion called for iodine. It gave a fine sting.

Mrs. Drack had left him a note on the kitchen table. It said, "Your supper is on the kitchen table. Don't dirty up."

That was all. No "Dear Marco" or "Love and kisses." Mrs. Drack had no time for such things. The note was propped up against a bowl holding Marco's supper.

"Thank you, Mrs. Drack," he said. "I'd never have found it without your excellent directions."

It was a bum joke and his voice sounded too loud in the empty apartment. Mrs. Drack was not much company, but she was better than no company at all, and Marco was one boy who liked company. He wished she were here so she could take him to the parade tonight. But she wasn't, and, anyhow, he knew that, even if she were, she wouldn't.

Opening the *States-Item,* he sat down to the cold supper. It was, as usual, leftover oatmeal from breakfast. He ate slowly, checking the closing prices on the New York Stock exchange. He owned no stocks, but that didn't mean he never would.

When he had finished eating, he washed the bowl and spoon (which is what Mrs. Drack meant by "Don't dirty up"). Then he went into his father's bedroom to call the police station.

If it wasn't for the telephone, Marco thought, he and his father would almost be strangers. The Old Man—as Marco called his father with the greatest respect and affection— seemed to be always at the police station. This, Marco guessed, was the way it was with policemen, like .45-caliber bullets received in the line of duty.

Long, long ago, when he was about eight, Marco used to go down to visit his father at the police station. The Old Man was always glad to see him but always busy. Marco would go into the firehouse next door and talk to the friendly firemen, who were seldom busy. He would slide down the pole and play with the firehouse dog, a big white one with black spots like splattered ink. (His name was Spot.) Marco would put on a fire helmet and sit in a fire truck and ring the big bell. And every time Spot would jump up into the seat beside him. That dumb dog never did learn he wasn't going to a fire.

It had been fun way back then, but now he was eleven.

Sitting on his father's hard bed, he dialed the police station.

"Hello, Dad," he said, for he recognized his father's deep, warm voice when he answered.

"No, this is Audubon Park Zoo, Mr. Wolf speaking," his father said. For *he* had recognized Marco's voice. Marco held the telephone at arm's length as a howl came through the earpiece.

"*Awr-awr-O-o-o-o-o-o!*"

He was some kidder, that father of his! Sometimes Marco felt as though he was the father and the Old Man was the son.

"Dad, let's try to be serious," he said. "And don't give me that business about 'You be Frank and I'll be Ernest.' I've got very important news."

"Shoot," his father said.

"This afternoon, on my route, I happened to meet and make friends with a tiger."

"That's fine," his father said. Oh, he was a kidder!

"I'm serious," Marco insisted.

"I'm a monkey's uncle."

"Dad, I mean it. He's a Royal Bengal."

"The best kind," his father said. "I wouldn't have any other."

Well, Marco thought, what're you gonna do? It was clear that the Old Man took him no more seriously than the Chief had. From the noise, Marco could tell that the police station was very busy, as it always was on parade nights, so he said good-by and started on his homework.

When Mrs. Drack came home from a jolly afternoon spent among the big stone tombs of St. Louis Number Three, topped off with a musical comedy at the Joy Theater, Marco was sound asleep.

4

MARCO PUTS IT IN WRITING

When Marco came into the kitchen next morning his breakfast was waiting for him. So was Mrs. Drack. Neither had changed from the last time Marco had seen them. They never did.

Breakfast was oatmeal. There had been a day—just five weeks ago—when Marco had liked oatmeal, with milk and brown sugar and a big chunk of butter like a gold nugget melting in the middle. But oatmeal seven mornings a week—and at night, too—five weeks in a row, is too much of a good thing.

After a couple of weeks of this, Marco, one morning, had said, softly and slowly, "Mrs. Drack, I simply cannot eat another spoonful of oatmeal."

"Of course you can" she had said. "All boys like oatmeal for breakfast."

"Not this boy," Marco had said.

"Boys need something that sticks to their ribs."

"How about sticking some ham and eggs to my ribs?" Marco had asked. "Say, how about that, Mrs. Drack?"

He might have used a bad word.

"And dirty up a skillet? Eat that oatmeal or do without!"

For a week Marco had done without. But he had found that around eleven o'clock in the morning he started to wobble quite a lot and to bump into all kinds of things.

He had gone back to the oatmeal.

On this particular Friday morning, he ate it slowly, watching the housekeeper, who stood by the stove, nodding her head.

"All boys like oatmeal," she said. "Sticks to their ribs."

Mrs. Drack was about forty years old, or even older. She was tall and bony. Her face and arms were rough and red, as if she scrubbed herself with the steel wool she used on the pots. When her long red mouth smiled, it was as if it cost her money. She had dyed black hair that was tied back and then hung down long and straight, like a pirate flag. Her hips were big and sharp and stuck out like a cow's as she leaned against the stove with her red arms folded across her chest, watching with her mean little eyes as Marco ate his oatmeal.

"You know something, Mrs. Drack?" he asked. "You know? I've got a tiger to play with!"

He might not have spoken at all.

"Perhaps you didn't hear me, Mrs. Drack, I say again, I've got a real live tiger for a friend. Royal Bengal. Ten-four?"

"Eat your oatmeal," Mrs. Drack rasped, "or there's going to be war."

"Really," Marco said. "Yesterday I just happened to come upon him on my route. And as soon as I finish throwing papers today, I'm going to pay him another visit."

"You're not paying anyone another anything unless you finish that oatmeal after I dirtied up a pot."

"Right you are, Mrs. Drack," Marco said. "Now about that tiger—"

"Never mind that tiger!" she yelled. "Where'd you get the skinned nose?"

"The tiger," Marco murmured.

She snorted. "Sticking your nose in other people's business, I bet."

Marco had taken aboard all the oatmeal he could handle. He laid down his spoon.

"And just what do you think you're doing, may I ask?" Mrs. Drack roared. She sounded like a .50-caliber machine gun in the little kitchen. "If you think for one single instant that I dirtied up a pot just to turn around and throw the food out—then, little boy, you need your head examined!"

Of course the oatmeal was never thrown out. Whatever was left over, Mrs. Drack served cold to him for supper. But one of the main reasons why Marco had decided he didn't like that lady was because she called him "little boy."

"Don't worry, Mrs. Drack," he said. "It won't be wasted." An idea had just popped into his head.

"It better not, or there's going to be war—that's all I can say."

It occurred to Marco as he picked up his schoolbooks that about all the housekeeper *did* say had to do with oatmeal, the eating of it or the pot it came out of.

Or war.

"Well, good-by, Mrs. Drack," Marco called. "Nice talking to you."

"Hmm."

"I'll see you this evening."

"Hmm."

The door slammed shut. Marco bowed low to it. Then he started down the stairs, humming a bouncy tune he made up as he went along.

"Now, ladies and gentlemen," Sister Helen Grace told the fifth-grade class, "for English today we're going to write a composition. (Groans.) It can be about anything that has happened to us or interests us. Remember, we must watch our spelling and punctuation. (Louder groans.) Start writing. . . . Start!"

Everyone began to write as if in a race. At the top of the paper they all put their names. Then they skipped a line and wrote "English."

Then most of them stopped and looked at the paper as if it were the first time they had ever seen such a thing. Then they looked at each other. Then they looked out the window.

Three girls and two boys tiptoed up to Sister, asking to

go to the drinking fountain. Silently, sternly, she pointed to their seats. In the back row, Peter Edgar Masters drew a skull and crossbones on the back of his hand and showed it to Wallie Olsen.

But Marco paid no attention to any of this. His mind was far away. For his title he wrote, "How I Found My New Friend."

Then, writing as rapidly as the pen would move across the paper, he described everything that had happened yesterday, starting with the big door at 420 Royal and how it opened when he had said, "Please." He knew Sister would like that—she often said that "please" was a magic word— but also it was a point that had caused him a good deal of wonder.

He left nothing out, giving a whole paragraph to the two doors in the courtyard and how he had tried to decide which one to open. He had just finished telling how he had gone back to be sure the tiger really was there when the bell rang.

Marco wrote, "After I finish throwing papers today I'm going to visit my New Friend and bring Him a nice surprise."

Then he wrote "The End" and put five lines underneath.

Gathering the sheets together, he was amazed that there were so many. He started to take the composition up to Sister's desk. There was a line of children ahead of him. He was tired from his labors—but happy. His left hand was particularly tired, since he was lefthanded.

He had almost reached Sister's desk when a sudden thought hit him like a blow.

He could not—he could not possibly hand in the composition.

If everyone knew about Tiger, that would be the end of

him. Someone with a big mustache would rush over there with a high-powered rifle and shoot him down, because this is what people always seemed to do with unusual stray animals, for some reason. The killer would be a big hero. His picture would be in the papers, and he would be on TV.

Marco could hear the man. He would be saying, "I was using a .338 Winchester Magnum with telescopic sights. My first shot was a trifle low. It caught the beast in the front paw. . . ."

Marco felt tears in his eyes. Oh, Marco, he thought, banging his fist against his forehead. What is wrong with you? Your brain is small! Small! SMALL!

It was bad enough that he had wanted to tell the world about the tiger, even though no one would believe him. But now he had it in writing.

If he handed in the composition, it was good-by, Tiger.

Ahead of him now were only Mary Jo Williams and Johnny Bill Green. Then no one was ahead of him but Sister. She had a round, pink, smiling face. "Well, Marco," she said, "you managed to produce quite a manuscript."

"Please, Sister," Marco begged, "let me give you another composition Monday. This one's no good."

"I'm sorry, Marco," she said, "but I must insist upon this one."

Marco had one end of the composition, she the other. Both were tugging. The class, on the way to lunch, crowded in the doorway, watching and listening happily. There were those who said Marco was Sister's pet. This was not true. It was just that Sister liked Marco and he liked her. Still it was sweet to see them fighting.

Sister Helen Grace's face was rounder and pinker than ever, but it was no longer smiling. Because she was his teacher and because he liked her and because she gave a quick jerk, Marco let her have the composition.

"All right, take it," he said grimly. "But only on one condition—you must promise to burn it as soon as you've read it."

"Marco Fennerty, Junior, I won't promise anything of the kind!" Sister exclaimed.

"Please, Sister!"

She jabbed her finger toward the door.

Marco knew when he was licked. He bowed, clicking his heels. Then, shoulders squared and a gallant smile on his face, he pushed through the crowd and started the long, lonely walk down the hall to the lunchroom.

"Good-by, Tiger," he said softly.

"Hey, Marco!" someone called. "Hey, hey, what's wrong with your nose, hey? Is that a hurt or dirt?"

"Both," Marco snapped.

Lunch was red beans and rice, a dish he really liked. But today it might as well have been stewed beetles and worms.

The class was at the end of arithmetic that afternoon when Marco suddenly had a vision of that man with the big mustache carefully aiming his rifle. . . .

Marco leaned back in his seat, threw back his head, and went, *"Um-ow-w-w-w-uhn-n-n-UGH!"*

In the desk ahead, Betty Burton blasted off, hung in mid-air for a moment, then—big for her age—landed with a crash that shook the classroom. Johnny Bill Green, trying to slip a note to Mary Jo Williams, gave it instead to Sandra Jacks.

"What," Sister Helen Grace demanded, "was THAT!"

Slowly, painfully, Marco raised his hand.

"That's the way tigers yawn," he said.

Everyone was staring at him—everyone but Sandra

Jacks, who was smiling at Johnny Bill Green as she folded his note.

"How do *you* know how tigers yawn?" Betty Burton asked, glaring at Marco.

He didn't want to lie, so he just ignored the question. "Of course," he said, "a real tiger does it much better."

"Oh, *sure!*" Betty Burton said.

Sister Helen Grace clapped her hands twice. "Class?" she said. "Class? There will be no more tiger yawns. Ever!"

"Yes, Sister," the class chorused, for she looked as though she meant it.

When the final bell rang, Sister stood at the door, handing back the compositions. As she gave Marco his, she had a curious look on her round pink face that was somewhat like a smile and somewhat like a frown.

Marco did not unfold the composition until he was two blocks away. The first thing he saw was the grade:

A—

Then, at the bottom of the last sheet, he found Sister's note:

> You have a vivid imagination and a flair for writing. See Stockton, Francis Richard, "The Lady or the Tiger?" Watch spelling and punctuation.

5

TIGER TALK

Usually, it took Marco an hour to cover his route, from the time he picked up his bundle at the substation until he had thrown the last paper. This afternoon, he was done in forty-two minutes flat. He barreled home, charged up the stairs, threw open the door, and ran inside, holding his arms out and whistling like a jet.

"Announcing the arrival of Flight Fifty-three from Calcutta, India!"

The apartment was silent.

Mrs. Drack, bless her heart, was back on Canal Street, or enjoying a movie or a graveyard. Marco got the leftover oatmeal and rushed out. There was the look of a storm to the south. Heavy blue clouds were moving in from the Gulf of Mexico, like a fleet of enemy warships. If it rained tonight, he thought, they would have to cancel the parade.

By the time Marco got to 420 Royal, he was so out of breath he could barely give the Open Sesame (if that's what it was). But when he turned the knob, the door swung open.

The tiger heard him coming and was making tiger noises long before his visitor got to his room. Marco set the bowl down and opened the door. The tiger came out faster than yesterday. He came out so fast, in fact, that he almost knocked the boy down.

"Hello, Tiger," Marco said in his low voice.

The tiger rubbed up against him—and almost knocked him down again.

Then the tiger sat on his haunches and waved his right paw in the air. Marco shook it. Then the tiger rolled over. Then he played dead, with all four paws in the air and his furry white belly showing. Then he ran around and around the courtyard as fast as three legs would carry him. Then, suddenly, he stopped and bunched together and then shot out, leaping high over the big concrete flowerpot in the middle of the patio.

And finally he sat up straight, his two front paws hanging in the air and his great yellow eyes on Marco's as he went, "Ho! Ha! Ah! Hah!"

The boy was delighted.

" 'Atta tiger, Tiger!" he said. "I knew you could do those tricks if you just put your mind to it. Look, I brought you something."

He put the bowl down before him. Tiger gave him a quick look. Then he padded up to the bowl and gave it a suspicious sniff. His mouth opened just enough for his tongue to flick out and into the bowl.

He looked around at Marco, as if to say, "Well, well, well!"

Then his long tongue rolled out like a red carpet and finished off the oatmeal in three licks.

"All tigers like oatmeal," Marco said. "Sticks to their ribs."

The empty bowl went clattering around the patio, with the tiger right behind it, walloping it with his tongue.

"All right, Tiger." Marco grabbed up the bowl before it got broken. "Now we're going to have a chat. Sit down, won't you?"

The tiger sat on his haunches. Marco sat on the edge of the fountain, crossing his legs. The tiger waited politely for him to begin.

"Now then . . ." Marco said.

He uncrossed his legs and crossed them the other way. He made a tent of his fingers. Then he hummed a little tune. How to begin? How do you talk with a tiger who can't talk?

Gungah! Like so many other things in life, this looked easy until you tried it.

But Marco was not discouraged. He knew he would have to do all the talking. This didn't bother him too much. It was, he thought, like having a chat with a large, hairy Frenchman who could say only *"Oui"* and *"Non"* and whatever a Frenchman might say (you could never be sure *what* a Frenchman might say) for "I don't know."

The problem was to find out how the tiger said these things.

"Now then, Tiger," Marco began. "Unless you particularly want to go into it, I think we can skip certain background information, such as exactly where you were born and how many brothers and sisters you had and whether yours was a happy childhood or not. Agreed?"

The tiger cocked a furry white eyebrow.

"By which," Marco said, trying to hold down his excitement, "you mean, 'Yes.' Correct?"

The tiger cocked his eyebrow.

"Now you're talking, Tiger! Now you're talking!"

There was a rumble that Marco thought at first was thunder. Then he realized it was the tiger's stomach.

"Still hungry, Tiger?" he asked.

Cocked eyebrow. Very cocked eyebrow.

"We'll have a snack as soon as we finish here," Marco said. "Tell me, Tiger, how do you like New Orleans?"

The tiger looked at Marco, then he looked at the sky. Tiger or no tiger, he had the saddest eyes Marco had ever seen.

Of course! What he had noticed about those eyes the first time was that they had no cruelty—only sadness. In the corner of the left eye was what looked very close to a tiger tear.

"I withdraw the question," Marco said. "Let me put it another way. Do you like New Orleans?"

The tiger's right ear twitched. A special, on-purpose twitch.

"Does that mean, 'No,' Tiger?" Marco asked.

The tiger stretched his long striped neck.

"*Hmm,*" Marco said. "I must admit I'm a bit confused at this point. I can't be sure whether you're answering my questions or just twitching your ears and stretching your neck. Are you answering my questions, Tiger?"

The tiger cocked his eyebrow.

"Thank you. And when you stretch your neck, does that mean, 'No'?"

Cocked eyebrow.

"And when you twitch your right ear, does that mean, 'Yes and no' or 'So-so'?"

Cocked eyebrow.

Marco slapped the tiger on his muscular shoulder.

"Tiger," he said, "we've got it made!"

The long white whiskers on the left side of the tiger's face jerked. Marco thought he was about to sneeze. . . . But he didn't sneeze.

"Now if I understand you," Marco said, "you don't dislike New Orleans."

Cocked eyebrow.

"But you don't particularly like it?"

Tiger sat still. His eyebrow didn't cock, his right ear didn't twitch, his neck didn't stretch. Then his whiskers jerked again.

Marco took a deep breath.

"It's not ... You think ... The thing is ... Oh, what am I trying to say, Tiger?"

Tiger's tail went *whap, whap, whap* against the flag-stones. So now Marco knew how he said, "I don't know." Still that didn't help much in learning his feelings about New Orleans.

Then Marco snapped his fingers.

"It's a nice place to visit but you wouldn't want to live here!"

He watched the tiger's eyebrow. But it didn't move. Ditto neck. Ditto ear. Ditto tail.

Then once more the left whiskers jerked.

"I'm afraid we're in trouble again," Marco said. "And really, Tiger, I can't see that you're doing much to help."

Tiger looked bored. No one, hard as he might try, can look as bored as a bored tiger. But somehow Marco got the feeling that it was not the tiger who was lying down on the job but Marco Fennerty, Junior.

For the fourth time the tiger's whiskers jerked.

"If you're going to sneeze, sneeze," the boy said. "You're making me nervous."

Tiger didn't sneeze.

"Are you trying to tell me something?"

The eyebrow, still for so long, cocked up into the top of Tiger's forehead.

It took some doing, but, after many questions, Marco figured out what the tiger was saying.

"When you jerk your whiskers like that," he said, "you mean, 'Not really,' or 'I wouldn't say that.' Right?"

Cocked eyebrow! Cocked eyebrow! Cocked eyebrow!

"Hurray!" Marco yelled.

The tiger came over and rubbed up against him. Clearly he was being petted. Tiger was telling him what a clever little fellow he was, to be sure.

They both breathed a huge sigh of relief. Marco uncrossed his legs, then recrossed them. The tiger lowered one paw and raised the other.

"Tell me something, Tiger," the boy said. "This has been bothering me for a good while now. Why do you always carry one paw in the air? Why do you do that?"

He looked at the tiger, waiting for an answer. The tiger looked at him, waiting for a more intelligent question. "Oh, of course," Marco cried. "How silly of me! Now then, do you go on three legs because you're giving one a rest?"

Tiger's whiskers jerked out, *I wouldn't say that.*

"I see, I see," Marco said, though he wasn't sure he did. "It isn't by any chance because you think it's the thing to do?"

Tiger gave him a scornful stretch of the neck.

"No, no, of course not," Marco said. "I shouldn't even have asked that."

Boy questioning, animal signaling his answers, they worked it out. The tiger always used three legs because he could see no good reason for using four when three would do just as well. He was that type of tiger.

In reply to Marco's questions, Tiger indicated that he liked New Orleans all right—what he had seen of it. But he missed being able to watch the sun come up and go down and having the stars spread over him at night. Also, he was always hungry and liked people

Marco rubbed his sore nose, swallowed, and asked, "To eat?"

Patiently the tiger stretched his long neck. No, not to eat. For company? Cocked eyebrow. Yes, for company. He also liked other tigers. He was very lonely cooped up in his quarters all the time, like some wild animal.

"How long have you been here?" Marco asked.

There went that tail again, *whap, whap, whap.*

"I'm sorry," the boy said. "I forget tigers can't tell time. But anyway, I'm sure you want to go back to the jungle."

In a long series of neck stretchings, tail whappings, eyebrow cockings, ear twitchings, and whisker jerkings, the tiger showed he would like that fine. But he was perfectly willing to settle for less. Life, he had found, was a series of compromises.

The main thing he wanted, he told Marco, was a better deal.

The boy looked at Tiger long and hard.

"I'll fix you up," he said quietly. "How, I don't know, but will—I'm eleven! I promise you, Tiger."

Marco put his hand out to the tiger. Tiger put his paw out to Marco. They shook on it.

There was a rumble that Marco thought was Tiger's stomach. But it was thunder.

"It's going to rain, Tiger," Marco said. "Rain hard. Do you like rain?"

Cocked eyebrow.

"Lightning?"

Twitched ear.

"Me, too," the boy said. "I can take it or leave it alone. How about thunder?"

Cocked eyebrow.

Marco beamed at him. "You're just like me, Tiger!" he cried. "I love thunder!"

The tiger didn't *love* it exactly. He was quiet by nature, but he looked forward to storms because, when it thundered, he could roar out his unhappiness, and the neighbors would not hear him and complain. The roars helped his spirits. In the close space of his room, though, they were pretty hard on the old ears. And a tiger really counted on his ears.

Then, from the street there came the merry jangle of bells and Marco jumped up. "Snack time, Tiger! Don't move. I'll be right back."

He ran out to the street and stopped the popsicle man, who was pedaling by on his bicycle cart.

"What do you suggest for a . . . a large animal?" Marco asked slyly.

The popsicle man gave a quiet groan and glanced up at the clouds sliding together overhead.

"Look, kid," he said, "I've got red ones and blue ones

and green ones and orange ones. Also banana, root beer, fudge sicles, pineapple and coconut. Take your pick."

Coconut was the closest to the jungle. It was also Marco's favorite flavor. He bought a coconut popsicle and asked the man to break it in half.

The popsicle man groaned louder, glancing up at the sky again. But he broke the popsicle. Then he started to pedal down the street as if Indians were after him.

When the boy got back to the courtyard, Tiger sat like a statue. "Don't move," Marco had said, and move he hadn't. They sat as before, Marco holding his half in one hand and Tiger's in the other, both of them licking away and nodding to each other from time to time as if saying, "Good, eh?" and "That's for true!"

Tigers can't purr like cats because they're not built that way. But if this tiger could have, he would have.

It was at this point that the front door opened and someone started to come through the carriageway. Marco and Tiger looked at each other, then back at the carriageway. It was so dark there that Marco could barely see. But the person was tall and a man. He was moving slowly and silently.

The tiger stopped licking his half of the popsicle. He lifted his upper lip from his big white fangs and went, *"Ah-r-r-r-r!"*

6

MAN-TO-MAN TALK

The man came out of the darkness into the patio.

He was a thin, old man, dressed in a loud checked sport coat, gray slacks, and rubber-soled shoes. Instead of a tie, he wore a bright red scarf around his throat.

His hair was pure white and he had more than his share of it. His ears were large and furry. His eyes were just a couple of eyes, kept apart by a nose. The nose is what held Marco's attention. It was the biggest and reddest nose the boy had ever seen.

Now *there*, Marco thought, is a nose!

"Perry?" he called. "Is that you?"

"In the flesh," Mr. Perry answered. "And who might you be, may I ask?"

"Marco Fennerty, Junior, sir."

"What are you doing here, Fennerty?" Mr. Perry asked. He had decided that, if Marco was going to call him Perry, he would call the boy Fennerty.

"Collecting for the *States-Item*."

As generous as nature had been in other ways, it had given Mr. Perry one of those little mouths that get even littler whenever the owner is upset. Mr. Perry's mouth was so little now that he might as well have had no mouth at all.

"If you'll pardon me for saying so, it doesn't look like

that at all, you know," he said, coming closer. "It looks to me as though you're feeding my tiger a coconut popsicle."

Marco had to admit it did look that way. He got to his feet. Mr. Perry, he noticed, was holding something wrapped in newspaper.

"Do you have any identification?" Mr. Perry asked. "Driver's license? Social Security card? Anything like that?"

"No, sir."

"I could have you arrested for breaking and entering, you know, Fennerty."

"Entering, yes, Perry. Breaking, no," Marco said. As the son of a policeman, he had a rather nice feel for such matters.

Between them, he and the tiger had finished off the popsicle by now. As if he had just remembered something, the tiger gave another low growl.

"I've brought you something, Rajah," Mr. Perry said.

He opened up the paper, which contained a sorry pile of gleaming white, meatless bones. Setting it down, he stepped back very quickly.

The tiger went slouching over to the bones and sniffed them without much enthusiasm.

"Popsicle spoiled his appetite," Mr. Perry said. Marco looked at the sky. The tiger growled.

"We never have really got along, you know," Mr. Perry said. "But then, who does with tigers?"

"Me," Marco said softly.

"Let me give you a word of warning," Mr. Perry said. "You know—

> "There was a small boy from Niger,
> Who smiled as he rode on a tiger.
> They came back from the ride
> With the small boy inside,
> And a smile on the face of the tiger."

"That's good, that's good!" Marco cried. "Did you write that?"

"Well," Mr. Perry said with a wave of his hand.

"I write a bit myself," Marco admitted shyly. "Compositions—that sort of thing."

"You're pretty small to have a paper route, you know, Fennerty," Mr. Perry said. "How old are you?"

"I just made eleven."

Mr. Perry stood with his arms folded across his chest and his head cocked back.

Marco stood facing Mr. Perry with his arms folded across his chest and his head cocked back. He liked to be called by his last name and was pleased that Perry thought he knew everything. This Perry really was okay. Obviously he had something on his mind, though what the boy had no idea.

"Do you have a work permit?" Mr. Perry asked in his nasal twang.

"No, sir," Marco answered. "I took the route over from Nathan Trowbridge when he retired. He's in the eighth grade at my school. I pay Na—I pay Trowbridge 50 per cent of the profits."

"This Trowbridge sounds like quite a lad," Mr. Perry said.

Standing there in the courtyard with their arms folded across their chests and their heads cocked back, the boy and the man talked for some time. Marco kept trying to bring the tiger into the conversation, but no go. The tiger just sat and listened—or seemed to listen.

"Let an old man give you a word of advice, Fennerty," Mr. Perry said. "Don't neglect your education. That has been my trouble from the start. Oh, I've always been able to do a lot of different things, but nothing really well. Am I getting across to you?"

"I think so, sir."

"I've worked in dime stores, handing out free samples of toothpaste and gumdrops—Rajah had no use for the former, loved the latter. I've sold vacuum cleaners door to door. I've demonstrated yo-yos on the street corner—the usual odd jobs, you know."

Marco nodded understandingly. The jobs *were* rather odd.

"For a while one time I sold sets of the encyclopedia. That's how I got Rajah. I took him and his cage in payment for a set of books from a man in the circus."

Oh, ho, Marco thought. At least I was right about the circus part!

Opening the door next to the tiger's quarters, Mr. Perry showed Marco the cage. It had been a beautiful thing once— gold with silver bars and huge red wheels, a cage any tiger would have been proud to call home. But now most of the paint had fallen off, and the bars were lumpy with rust. It had been a beautiful thing once, but that had been long, long ago.

"Why did you want a tiger anyhow, Perry?" Marco asked. He knew why *he* would want one. But he was he, not Perry.

Slowly, thoughtfully, Mr. Perry closed the big wooden door and latched it. Then he turned and looked at Marco.

"How many people do you know personally who own tigers, Fennerty? Think now and don't answer too quickly."

Marco thought of Sister Helen Grace, the Chief, Miss Allen at the library, all the policemen, the kids at school. Of course he didn't know a mess of people, but not one of them owned a tiger.

"I see what you mean, Perry," he said.

"You see? You see?" Mr. Perry was excited. "I had something that nobody else had. I didn't go around shooting my mouth off about it, but every once in a while, when things were really looking black, I could say to myself, 'I am the proud owner of a Royal Bengal tiger.' You see?"

Marco said he saw.

Behind them, the tiger yawned. *"Um-ow-w-w-ughn-n-n-UGH!"*

Mr. Perry jumped what Marco guessed—whenever he thought about it later, which was often—must have been a good three feet straight up.

"I would much prefer he didn't do that, you know," Mr. Perry said when he came down.

After he had first got the tiger, he told Marco, he had been very fortunate in finding work. But for some time now he had been having bad luck. It was getting hard to feed himself, let alone the tiger.

Marco decided that this would be a good time to remind Perry why he was here. Mr. Perry's mouth almost disappeared, but he paid up.

"What are you going to do about the tiger?" Marco asked, writing out a receipt.

"The best answer I can give you, Fennerty, is I don't know," Mr. Perry said. "That's the best answer I can give you."

"How much would it cost to send him back to India?" Marco wanted to know. "I'll be glad to chip in with you."

"Let's be practical, Fennerty," Mr. Perry said. "Neither of us will ever have that kind of money."

"I will," Marco said quietly.

Mr. Perry gazed at him a moment. "Yes, Fennerty, I believe you will—but not if you stick with the newspaper game, you know."

"That's how I got Rajah. I took him and his cage in payment for
a set of books from a man in the circus."

"I don't suppose you'd want to donate him to the Audubon Park Zoo," Marco said without much enthusiasm.

His father had taken him out there on the St. Charles Avenue streetcar a couple of Sundays when the fishing was bad. It had struck Marco as quite a fine, upstanding zoo. The animals seemed to get enough to eat and they lived out in the open. Tiger could sleep under the stars.

But he could not stand the thought of Tiger behind bars, pacing up and down like a convict in his old-time striped prison suit. No! Tigers were meant to be free.

"Not that he would want to live in a zoo," Marco added.

"My guess is that Rajah would like it fine," Mr. Perry said. "But the zoo wouldn't take him."

Marco was outraged. "Wouldn't take him!" he yelled. "And why NOT?"

"Age," Mr. Perry said. "Rajah's a tiger past his prime."

"No."

"Yes."

"He can't be."

"He is," Mr. Perry said. "See the long white hair on his cheeks? See how worn down his teeth are? See all his scars? See how dull his coat is?"

"Yes," Marco agreed softly to each question, "yes, yes, yes."

"These are all signs of age, you know, Fennerty," Mr. Perry said. Clearly he had been studying up on tigers and wanted to show off a bit.

"Your Royal Bengals have much finer coats than tigers from China and Siberia, you know. But even your Royal Bengal will start to fade after a while."

Marco felt a great lump in his throat. *My* Royal Bengal, he thought. Oh, if he really were mine!

He had not noticed the scars before, but Tiger had them, and plenty of them. Also, Marco had to admit, the coat could have had more of a shine. It looked like a very expensive coat that Tiger had sent to the dry cleaners once too often.

"Rajah," Mr. Perry said, "is twenty if he's a day. And for a tiger that's getting on, you know. After twelve, they start to lose their market value."

There just didn't seem to be anywhere for old tigers. Marco and Mr. Perry stood in silence. The tiger looked from Marco to Mr. Perry and back to Marco again. Then, with a long, sad groan, he lay down with his head on a great paw.

"We've go to do something, you know," Mr. Perry said. "I just came home this evening to bring Rajah his supper and throw a few things in a bag. You can stop the paper, by the way. A man's giving me a ride to the West tonight. Maybe in the West my luck with change." He paused, then asked, "You want him?"

Marco's heart leaped in his chest. Gungah! But then he shook his head sadly. "Our landlord won't let us have pets."

"Even a cat?" Mr. Perry asked. "The meanest landlord will usually let you have a cat. And he's nothing in the world but a big cat, you know."

"Well, Perry, I could speak to my father," Marco said —without much hope.

"Do that, Fennerty. You do that. You're a serious-minded chap, with a regular job—not like the blubberheads one sees so often nowadays who care only for pleasure, with never a thought for tomorrow. It's obvious you two get along, and I know you'll give him a good home."

"We'll see," Marco said. He put the tiger in his quarters and latched the door. Then he picked up the bowl with his left hand and shook hands with Mr. Perry with his right.

"Good-by, Perry," he said. "Good luck out West."

"Thank you, Fennerty," Mr. Perry said. "Pleased to have made your acquaintanceship."

"Good-by, Tiger," Marco called.

From behind the door there came a friendly growl.

As soon as Marco got home he telephoned his father at the police station. "Dad, remember the tiger I told you about yesterday?"

"Of course. How could I forget?"

"Well, today the owner said I could have him."

"Really? What a break!"

"Then I can have him?"

"Of course. Can't turn something like that down."

"Dad, I'm serious."

"Glad to know you, Serious. Fennerty here."

Oh, he was some kidder, that Old Man of his. He sure was!

7

MRS. DRACK HAS A SURPRISE

Marco tried to do his homework but couldn't get anywhere. He kept tapping his pencil and thinking about Tiger. It would be impossible to keep him in the apartment, even if the landlord gave his permission—which he wouldn't. Not him. No, not him. Another thing, with Perry gone, Tiger could not stay much longer at 420 Royal.

In the distance, thunder boomed like a gun.

Again there came that vision of the man with the big mustache and the high-powered rifle. Marco shivered. Unless he did something—and soon—Tiger was as good as dead.

Why the man would have a mustache, Marco couldn't say. But he knew the fellow would have one, just as sure as he would have a rifle.

Marco tapped the pencil faster.

There was only one answer. Put Tiger on a ship bound for India. The Chief would be the guy to see about that. As an ex-Navy man, he would have the know-how. He would see the Chief first thing in the morning, Marco decided.

That matter settled nicely, he tore into the homework. He had just made a good start when Mrs. Drack came home. He could hear her banging around in the kitchen, singing.

Singing? *Mrs. Drack?*

"Well, well, madame," Marco said, strolling into the kitchen. "Have fun in the graveyard?"

She was wearing her silly little hat with the phony fruit. Actually, Marco thought, anything would look silly on her except one of those cocked hats that pirates wear.

"Oh, hello, Marco," she said. "I'll have your supper ready in a jiffy."

There was something about her voice. Where were those razor blades? Marco sat down at the table. In front of him a bunch of withered flowers—she must have lifted them off a tomb—sagged in a glass of water.

"I *wanted* to fix you a nice bowl of gumbo," she said.

"I know," Marco answered. Mrs. Drack always *wanted* to fix him a nice something-or-other but somehow never did.

"Tonight, we don't have time, though," she said. "And you'll have the oatmeal all ready in the morning."

"Time for what?" Marco asked warily.

Mrs. Drack turned from the stove with a smile. Marco had seen such a smile on kids at school when the wind had been knocked out of them.

"We're going visiting!" she exclaimed.

"No, we're not," he said.

"This friend of mine has a boy just about your age," she went on firmly. "Y'all can play together. Marco, they live in a shotgun!"

There might have been a time when that would have interested him. But Marco had learned that, in New Orleans, at least, a shotgun was a house in which all the rooms were in a straight line—fire a shotgun in the front door and blow the read end off.

"I'm not going," he said.

Mrs. Drack, somehow, was still smiling, but she was having trouble getting her words out. "Yes, you are, Marco my lad. Now, hurry up and eat your oatmeal so we can get started."

"Tell you what," Marco said brightly. "You run along. I'll look after things at this end."

The reason why Mrs. Drack was having trouble getting her words out was that she was talking through her big white teeth. They stretched across her red face like a tile wall.

"I have," she said. "Taken," she went on. "Just about," she added. "All," she told him. "I can STAND!"

"But, Mrs. Drack," Marco said. "I've got homework."

"I'll homework you, Marco Fennerty, if you don't hurry up and eat that oatmeal after I dirtied up a pot!"

Mrs. Drack's friend lived on Burgundy, just a few blocks away. Marco and the housekeeper walked up St. Ann to Burgundy. Rumbling and grumbling, the storm seemed to have moved off. But the evening was tight with a different kind of excitement.

A crowd was coming toward them. Soft-drink venders, a man with a cluster of bright balloons that looked as though they were about to lift him into the air, another man with a bushel basket filled with tiny bags of peanuts, and just plain people rushed past them, smiling, on the way to the parade. The boy looked at them longingly.

"Hey, you're going the wrong way!" the balloon man yelled.

"I know." Marco sighed.

"Go peddle your balloons, you," the housekeeper snapped, pulling Marco around the corner to the shotgun house.

Mrs. Drack's friend and three other ladies stood in a line along the wall of the front room. They were all huge. Standing there, waiting, they made Marco think of the old Indian game in which the captive had to run down the line and everyone would swat him with whatever was handy—he, of course, being the captive.

"How do you do, ma'am?" he said to each Indian.

"You're a fortunate lad to have someone like Mrs. Drack to look after you," the first one told him grimly. "Fortunate *indeed.*"

"Hear that?" Mrs. Drack demanded, with a jab in his left side.

"The boy's too skinny," the second said.

"Eats too many sweets," the third said.

"Eat?" Mrs. Drack cried. "He eats like a horse!"

"Yeah," Marco broke in. "Oats, oats, nothing but oats."

The fourth lady wore a hearing aid. "What did the boy say?" she asked. "Make him speak up!"

"I said—" Marco began. This time the right side got it.

"Never mind," Mrs. Drack said, glancing to where a card table and chairs were set up in the corner. "Let's get started. I'm feeling lucky tonight."

8

HERE COMES THE PARADE!

Marco was taken through the narrow, cheerless house and put—*pushed* was more like it—into the last room. The door shut behind him like the door of a prison cell.

Yet the room was not at all like a cell.

Gungah! He had never seen so many toys. The shelves on one wall were filled with soldiers, knights, Indians, Foreign Legionnaires, Arabs. Models of the *Bonhomme Richard, Old Ironsides, PT-109,* and other famous American fighting ships were in a line on another shelf.

There was a rowing machine behind the bed. From the ceiling in one corner, like a huge ripe grape, hung a punching bag. Also from up there prop planes dangled, along with jets and rocket ships—all slowly swinging in the air currents. . . .

Marco heard the clink of coins and Mrs. Drack's harsh voice.

"What did she say?" the lady with the hearing aid asked.

"I SAID," Mrs. Drack repeated, "I bet a SILVER DIME!"

From afar there came the wail of a police siren. It had a joyous sound, as sirens did only at Carnival time. The parade was coming.

Marco went over for a closer look at the ship models. They were—all of them—excellent jobs. Yet they seemed

to be there, like books in some people's homes, just for show. Carefully, he picked up the PT boat.

A long, bare, hairy arm reached over his shoulder and snatched the model out of his hands.

Marco whirled. The son of Mrs. Drack's friend had been crouching silently behind the door all the time, like a patient spider in its lair.

"I just wanted to see it," Marco said.

"No seas to it. All dry land."

"Please, can't I just see it?" Marco asked.

"No seas to it. All dry land."

The son of Mrs. Drack's friend had a vicious, whispery

voice. He put the model back on the shelf. He had a short, thick body, with long arms and legs. Beady eyes. Greasy black hair. He looked like a spider with a mess of limbs missing.

Marco put his hand out, saying, "I'm Marco Fennerty, Junior."

Spider pulled his own hand back. No seas there, either.

"What grade you in?" he demanded.

"Fifth," Marco said.

"Is *that* all!"

Yes, Marco admitted, that was all. Spider had the worldly-wise air of a sixth grader. Marco went over and took a swip at the punching bag. With an annoyed shake of his head, Spider grabbed the bag and held it still.

"Name the presidents of the United States and the years in which they served," he ordered.

"We haven't had that yet," Marco said. He sat down at the rowing machine and started to row, but Spider held the seat still with his foot.

In the distance, the siren called again. Then Marco could hear the *rum-da-da, rum-da-da-da-da* of drums. A band started to play. A thought came to him. He could get a throw for Tiger from one of the floats.

"Say, look, *amigo*," Marco suggested casually, "why don't you and I cut out and go watch the parade?"

"No, no, no." Spider shook that greasy head of his again. "Mama said that I should entertain you here." He stuck out a long pale finger at Marco: "Recite the Preamble to the Contitution of the United States."

"We haven't had that yet, either." Marco got up and took another swipe at the bag. Spider leaped over and grabbed it.

"You call yourself an American?"

"Yes, I do," Marco answered firmly.

"Then what are the first ten amendments to the Constitution called?"

Marco gazed at his host as he might at a roach. The music of the band came louder. The march sounded like—yes, it was "Dixie."

"The Bill of Rights, stupid!" Spider yelled. "Hey, how'd you get the bobo on your nose? And you've got 'em on your elbows, too. How'd you get all the bobos on your nose and elbows?"

For a delightful three seconds Marco considered telling Spider exactly how he had received the bobos on his nose and elbows. But then he shrugged his shoulders.

"Do you know *anything?*" Spider demanded.

"Yes, I do," Marco answered quietly. He held out his left hand. "See this?"

"Just an old hand. So what?"

Slowly Marco curled the fingers into a fist. "If," he said, still quietly, "you don't shut up that big mouth of yours, I'm going to take this and give you a bobo to remember. Follow me?"

Spider nodded, silent.

"I'm shoving off," Marco said. "Count to five hundred slow before you run tell your mama. Follow me?"

Spider nodded again.

"Don't follow me," Marco ordered. He took a round-house swing at the punching bag. It was still banging back and forth in a very satisfactory manner when he slipped out the kitchen door.

As he passed under the front-room window he heard the clink of silver. The lady with the hearing aid asked, "What did she say?"

"I SAID . . . !" Mrs. Drack shouted, but Marco was gone.

He ran down the dark, quiet street toward the noise and light of Royal. The sidewalks there were clogged with people. Fathers held children on their shoulders. One man had brought a stepladder, to the top of which was nailed an orange crate, containing three patient youngsters. A bald-headed man held a cigar box on the end of a long pole.

Taking up a position by the iron picket fence behind St. Louis Cathedral, Marco looked up the street. He could feel a fullness in his chest and his heart was pounding.

Day parades were fine during Carnival, but there was a special thrill, an enchantment all its own to a night parade.

A police car with a red blinker light on top was coming slowly along the street, the light flashing on the balconies filled with flowerpots and people. A clop of hoofs and the mounted police appeared, pressing the crowd back on each side.

Up the street, Marco could see the floats and the wandering fire of the flambeaux carriers. A high-school band, passing by, struck up "Dixie." The crowd cheered.

Then, here were the flambeaux carriers! They came trotting, prancing, dancing down the pavement, twirling their pink and white flares. Behind them were the huge floats, rocking along the narrow street like a herd of painted elephants, like a fleet of glittering battleships.

All around Marco outstretched hands went up in the Carnival salute and everyone shouted, "Throw me something, Mister!"

Marco's hand went up and his yell went out, but his hand was lost in the thicket of hands and his yell was drowned in the hurricane roar of the crowd. From the balconies came long paper streamers and blizzards of confetti.

The Carnival maskers on the floats were throwing trinkets up to the people on the balconies, down to the crowd on the street. All was a wild confusion of blinding lights and deafening sounds.

A string of beads came winging to Marco. He snatched at it, caught it, but the string broke and the beads exploded like bird shot against the fence. The first float passed.

The crowd was silent, saving its breath, except for the "Hup, two, three, four!" of the children as a marching unit went by. Then the second float approached, towed by a little red tractor. The hurricane roar went up again, and so did the hands. A throw came toward Marco. He reached for it. So did a long-armed woman. She caught it.

A band went by with a rattle of drums. The drum major blew his whistle and the band struck up "Dixie." The crowd went wild. Then came another float, and another, and another, the throws shooting off them like ack-ack. Marco stretched his hand out for one, but the baldheaded man snagged it with his cigar box.

"I'm sorry, Tiger," Marco whispered, although he could have shouted and no one would have heard in the yells and whistles and trumpet blasts and all that made up the song of the night parade.

There were only a few more floats. One passed, quickly followed by another. Then there was only one left. From some distant point, thunder, like a freight train, started a slow, rumbling journey toward Royal Street, picking up speed, coming along faster, louder . . . then banged overhead.

Raindrops smacked the sidewalk at Marco's feet, shining in the lights like brand-new dimes. The spots became as big as nickels, then quarters. The storm exploded with a white flash of lightning and a blast of thunder. The rain came down like a silver curtain, cold and wet. The crowd screamed a different scream than before.

The last float approached, throws flying. It passed by, rounding the corner at Orleans Street. The crowd was breaking up as if melted by the rain.

"Please," Marco whispered.

Sock! Something hit his palm and his fingers closed on it—a small rubber ball.

"Thank you," Marco whispered and ran home through the rain with the ball in his fist.

He charged up the staircase as if it were San Juan Hill. In the apartment, he ran to the closet and took out his father's yellow slicker and black rubber boots, the gear Sergeant Fennerty had worn as a traffic cop. The boots came up well past Marco's knees and the slicker dragged on the floor, but never mind.

In the bathroom, he gathered up a beach towel, two bath towels, and a hand towel, which just about wiped out the towel department in the Fennerty household. Thunder pounded on the roof with both fists. Rain rattled and hammered and sometimes came in solid blasts, as if someone were standing on the balcony outside, tossing pails of water against the bathroom window.

During the flashes of lightning, Marco saw that the patio was a lake, the raindrops making little fountains when they hit. The magnolia tree there was taking a terrible beating from the wind. Its branches creaked and whacked together, so that Marco was afraid they would snap off. He liked that tree.

He clapped a rain hat on his head and took a look at himself in the hall mirror. He looked pretty good. Then, rolling up the towels, he put them under the slicker and started down the stairs.

Outside, the wild, cold rain hit him in the face so hard it took his breath away. The street was a rushing black river, sweeping along the confetti and streamers and other mess left in the wake of the parade. Marco was the only one out walking—probably, he thought, the only one in the whole city.

From the river, the Mississippi River, unseen ships called to each other. The blare of their horns bounced off the brick buildings around him, echoing in the street, so that it seemed as though the ships had floated up over the wharf and were wandering around lost in the city.

Cars came swishing past like speedboats, shooting up a sheet of white water on each side. The raindrops made long yellow streaks in the headlights.

Did the people in those cars, Marco asked himself, look out their windows and wonder about the boy walking stiff-legged in the big rubber boots, with the yellow slicker trailing behind him—and something clutched in his fist? Where was he going? What strange mission took him out on a night like this?

Did they, Marco wanted to know, turn to each other in the warm, dry cars (with the radio playing soft music) and ask any of these questions?

Probably not.

No.

Nuts to them!

Most of the time on Royal Street Marco was walking under balconies that kept the rain off him pretty well. But sometimes the wind blew it in on him in great gusts, as if trying to even the score. Far ahead, through the black iron grillwork of other balconies. he could see lightning flickering and flashing on the tall white office buildings of downtown New Orleans.

Lightning glowed on the suits of armor and ran along the

blades of the swords in the antique shop windows. In one especially bright flash, a statue of Napoleon glared out at him. It gave him quite a scare. He squared his shoulders and went on.

At 420 Royal, he whispered "Please," and slipped inside the door. He went slowly, feeling his way along the rough bricks of the carriageway in the inky dark. Lightning blazed in the rain-whipped courtyard, with an awful crash just seconds behind.

But loud as the thunder was, Marco could hear over it the roar of his friend.

When he unlatched the door, the tiger came out slowly, one paw in the air as usual and shaking his head with a look on his long, sad face as though saying, "Whew!" He must have just about split his eardrums with that last roar. But he was glad to see the boy and showed it.

"Look, Tiger, I brought you something from the Carnival parade," Marco said. "It's supposed to be good luck to get a throw."

The tiger studied the ball, sniffed it, bit it carefully, then glanced at the boy as if to say, "Well, what d'yuh know about *that?*"

Marco rolled the ball into the carriage room. Then, side by side, the two buddies strolled up and down the flooded courtyard, with the rain beating down on them and the lightning flashing above them and the thunder booming around them. The rest of the world, Marco thought, must be awfully quiet and dry tonight.

He threw his arm around the tiger's rolling shoulders. "This is the stuff, hey, Tiger?"

"Ho!" the tiger growled. "Ha!"

Marco tried hopping on one leg, but the boot kept slipping off, so he just walked on two legs while the tiger went on

Sometimes, when it thundered, Marco threw back his head and tried a few roars of his own. But mostly he let Tiger solo.

three. Sometimes, when it thundered, Marco threw back his head and tried a few roars of his own. But mostly he let Tiger have a solo.

Even after the hubbub of the parade, the tiger's cries were something to hear. They prickled the hairs on the back of Marco's neck and made shivers run down his spine. They started with a low, throat-clearing growl that built up to a roar that filled the courtyard and seemed to frighten the thunderclaps away. They were wild and brave and mighty, loaded with anger, and yet they always ended on a note of the deepest sadness.

"You might think it's dangerous, Tiger, to be out amid the elements like this," Marco said, "but a person's chances of getting struck by lightning are one in a million. . . . A tiger's chances," he added thoughtfully, "might be even less."

Tiger gave no sign of having heard. But, between the thunder and the roars, Marco's ears were humming so that the boy was not sure he had spoken at all.

"Had about enough, Tiger?"

Tiger made no reply, and Marco couldn't be sure he had asked *that* either. But when he opened the door, the tiger went right into his room. Marco rubbed him down with the beach towel, then the bath towels, and finished off his great paws with the hand towel. In the glow of lightning, Marco could see him smile.

"Good night, Tiger," he said. "See you tomorrow."

Tomorrow! The big day.

9

THINGS ARE NOT AS THEY SEEM

"WAKE! WAKE! WAKE! WAKE! Wake-wake-wake-wake-wake-wake-wake!"

The cheery bird call woke Marco from a deep sleep next morning. He got out of bed and went to the window. It was still quite dark.

On the topmost branch of the magnolia in the patio there was a cardinal, fire-red with a black mask across his eyes, like someone at a Carnival ball. Usually, all Marco saw in the Quarter were pigeons and sparrows. The cardinal was a beautiful bird to have such a beautiful song. He was a rare bird.

He was bubbling over with his news that the storm had ended and a new day was about to begin.

"WAKE! WAKE! WAKE! WAKE! Wake-wake-wake-wake-wake-wake-wake!"

Then, apparently, the cardinal went back to sleep because Marco heard no further from him. The boy lay on his bed, waiting, feeling good from the call.

There had been a time, when he was five or so, that he had always waited in vain for tomorrow. It had always been today—and tomorrow was tomorrow. You had to go to bed and wake up . . . and then it would be tomorrow. But when you woke up it was today. And tomorrow was still tomorrow.

But now tomorrow was here. Saturday—the big day. Marco lay on his back, planning exactly what he would do on this day of days, watching the darkness drain out of his room as though through a hole in the corner. When the room seemed light enough, he jumped up and got dressed. Suddenly, the birds—all of them—started to sing.

Marco tiptoed past Mrs. Drack's closed door. He did not particularly care to see her right now. He had had enough of her and her war when he had come home last night.

The sound of serious snoring came from behind Mrs. Drack's closed door. It sounded as though she were sawing through the door. She even *snored* mad!

Quickly, quietly, Marco ate his cold oatmeal, then slipped out. The air had an exciting cleanness and freshness. He stepped along smartly, breathing deeply, humming a march he made up as he went along the shiny wet streets.

The Chief took awhile to answer his bell. But, finally, the buzzer sounded and Marco pushed open the street door. He climbed up the narrow stairs that smelled of food and cats—and maybe rats—to the second floor. The Chief was waiting in the doorway.

"Hey, Chief!"

"Hello, Marco."

The greeting, Marco thought, could have been just a bit heartier.

"Wake you?" he asked.

"No, indeed. Now what would I be doing, sleeping at this hour?"

"I've come for that cup of jamoke," Marco said.

"Great!" the Chief exclaimed. "Nothing like a cup of jamoke in the wee hours of the morning. By the way, Marco, what time *is* it?"

"Four bells," Marco told him. "0600."

The Chief stretched. "That late," he said.

He was wearing a white T-shirt that made his copper skin look that much darker. Marco was slightly disappointed to see no tattoos on his powerful, hairless arms.

As the Chief went into the kitchen to fix the jamoke, Marco studied the tiny front room. It was quite bare, as he had guessed it would be, with just a cot and a chair and a leather footstool. But on the wall was a big, brightly-colored painting of Custer's Last Stand.

It was, Marco thought, very fine indeed for a blind man to have such a thing on his wall.

They drank the jamoke from white pottery mugs at the kitchen table. The Chief had put three spoonfuls of sugar and a big slug of milk in Marco's. But the boy could still taste the strange, slightly-bitter, grownup flavor of the jamoke and he had a pretty good idea that what he was drinking was coffee.

The Chief drank his black. He put his copper nose, like the prow of a ship, over the mug and breathed in the aroma, smiling to himself.

"Chief, I got troubles," Marco began.

"Well, dog my cats!" the Chief said. "What's a fine lad like yourself doing, having troubles at—what did you say it was—four bells?"

"Remember the tiger I told you about?" Marco asked.

The Chief started to smile—or maybe yawn—and put his hand over his mouth. "Of course."

"Well, I'm trying to get him back to India," Marco explained.

"I see."

"And, though much can be said for air freight, I think the best way is by boat."

"I see."

"So I thought that, as an ex-Navy man, you could give

me some pointers on how to go about this," Marco went on. "Maybe even arrange for him to get a ride on the next Navy ship going that way."

"I see," the Chief said. "Marco, before we go any further, I think we should clear up one point. I'm not Navy."

"Not Navy!"

"Not Navy."

"You're not Navy," Marco murmured. "Then why do you have a bosun's whistle?"

The Chief took the whistle from his pocket and held it out to Marco in his big brown hand.

"It isn't," he said. "It's just a tin whistle made on an island in the Pacific. Namely Japan."

"Then why do they call you 'Chief'?"

The Chief pushed his mug aside and leaned across the table. Marco could feel those blind eyes boring into his head.

"How do you feel about Indians?"

"I don't know," Marco answered. "What do you mean, how do I feel about Indians?"

"Do you feel that the only good Indian is a dead Indian?"

"Not at all!" Marco cried. "I wish, that some of my best friends were Indians."

"I'm glad to hear you say that, Marco, and I'll tell you why. I'm three-fifths Cherokee."

"Really?" Marco asked. "Say, that's great!"

The Chief reached into his back pocket and pulled out his wallet. "Look," he said, handing the boy a bill. "I don't know exactly what your trouble is but maybe this will help."

"Hey, this is a five-dollar bill!" Marco exclaimed.

"I know."

"Thanks very much, Chief. Want a receipt?"

"That won't be necessary."

"I better get going," Marco said. "Got a mess of things to do today. Good-by, and thanks for the jamoke."

"Good-by, Marco. Good luck."

Marco did not say, "Thanks, I'll need it," because everyone said that. He just said, "Thanks." Back on the street, he continued his marching and humming. But his step was not so lively as before and the tune was no longer gay.

This was going to be harder than he had thought. Like learning how to whistle, or using bubble gum without ruining your face.

He stopped at a public telephone booth on the corner. He looked up a steamship company in the yellow pages, dropped a nickel in the slot, put his handkerchief over the mouthpiece and dialed the number.

"I'm calling to learn how much it would cost to ship a tiger from New Orleans to Calcutta," he said in his deepest voice.

The steamship man chuckled. "Surely you mean to ship a tiger from Calcutta to New Orleans."

"No, I want to ship him home," Marco explained. He felt something begin to crawl around inside him, like a small, cold snake.

"Well, if you say so." The man did not sound at all convinced. "The tariff rate for shipping livestock—cattle and all—is by the head."

"I'm just interested in a tiger," Marco pointed out.

"I know," the man said. "Let's see now . . . Tiger, tiger . . ."

Marco could hear the rustle of pages. The snake—or whatever it was inside him—had grown bigger, colder.

"Here we are," the man said. "The tariff rate for shipping

tigers is $376 per cubic meter. A cubic meter is a little more than thirty-five cubic feet. How many cubic feet does your tiger have—give or take a few cubic feet?"

"I don't know about that," Marco admitted. "He's got four feet, but he only puts three down."

"I'm afraid," the man said slowly, "that won't help us. How big is he—give or take a few inches?"

"He's more than ten feet long, from the tip of his nose to the tip of his tail."

"The tail rides free," the man put in.

"Fine and dandy!"

"But wait a minute," the man said. "We've got to figure this by the cage. The shipper—that's you—supplies the cage."

"I have one!" Marco cried, remembering the circus cage. Surely good ol' Perry meant for him to have that, too.

"How big is it—give or take a few inches?"

Marco rubbed his nose. "I don't know."

"Let's figure the average cage," the man said. "Twelve feet long by six feet wide by ten feet high. Give him a little space to move around in. Okay?"

"Fine and dandy. How much would that be?"

A large woman with a red face and arms like balloons waddled up to the booth and gave Marco a mean look. He held up one finger.

"Let's see now," the man said. Marco could hear the soft clatter of an adding machine. "The rates are high," the man admitted. "But you must remember, there's an element of risk. All sort of things can happen when you fool with animals at sea."

"How much, please?" Marco asked.

"Wait now," the man said. "You'll also have to pay one of

the crew to act as keeper. That would be, oh, say, sixty dollars. And the shipper supplies the food."

Marco smiled brightly at the woman. "How much food would it take?"

"Enough to last fifty-six to sixty-one days."

"*What?*"

"Look at your map, sir. India's halfway around the world. Calcutta's the last port in the service. After that, we start coming back."

"I see," Marco said. Fifty-six to sixty-one days! That would be a mess of oatmeal.

"We supply the water," the man pointed out.

"That's a break."

The large woman outside the booth tapped on the door with a finger like a weiner.

"How much would it cost me altogether?" Marco asked.

"You must understand," the man went on. "We take the animal only from port to port. Anything beyond that is the shipper's responsibility."

"Please, how much would it cost port to port?" Marco asked.

"From end of ship's tackle in New Orleans to King George Docks in Calcutta—$6,700."

Marco swallowed. "That much."

"Give or take a few dollars."

"That must be first class," Marco said.

"There's only one class for tigers, sir. And let's not forget the keeper's fee. Make that $6,760."

"Give or take a few dollars," Marco said.

"Give or take a few dollars," the man agreed. "Who is this calling, please?"

"Just a friend," Marco thanked the man and hung up. "Lovely day," he remarked to the large woman as he left the booth.

"Kids!" she muttered, stuffing herself inside like a bag of groceries.

As Marco walked along now there was no march left in him, and the tune was so sad he stopped humming. $6,760! And that was just to the dock at Calcutta. There would be other expenses before Tiger was back in the jungle. There were no two ways about it: He had to get hold of about $7,000.

Seven thousand bucks!

Of course he had the five dollars that the Chief had donated and his part of the carrier's share of the paper-route money. What this part would be, Marco hadn't bothered to work out. He had no head for figures—he was a poet, not a clerk—but whatever he had was just a drop in the bucket.

Seven thousand smackeroos. Gungah!

"Pralines? Praw-LEENS? Won't someone buy my nice pralines today?" A large Negro woman, wearing an apron and with her hair tied in a bright red bandanna was walking toward him slowly, carrying a shopping basket filled with the rich nutty candies.

Marco was sorely tempted to buy a couple—if Tiger liked popsicles and gumdrops, he would surely go for pralines— but this was no time to be getting reckless with money. He let the woman go on down the street, swinging her basket and chanting her sad song.

Nathan Trowbridge was lying in a hammock in the shade of a chinaberry tree when Marco came into the tiny patio. Nathan was smiling blissfully, hands clasped over a well-filled stomach, eyes closed.

No cold oatmeal for this vast thirteen-year-old. A six-ounce glass of chilled orange juice, followed by four large buckwheat cakes, with plenty of butter and syrup, surrounded by links of crisp pork sausage, the works washed down by two tall glasses of fortified milk—this had been breakfast for Nathan Trowbridge IV.

"Hi, Nathan," Marco said.

"Where y'at, man?" Nathan drawled. This was one New Orleans expression that particularly annoyed Marco.

"If you'd open your eyes, you would see where I'm at," he answered. He couldn't help it. He just didn't like his business partner. He was *some* bad. But today of all days, Marco had to be nice to Nathan.

"Taking a nap?" he asked.

"No, man, just lyin' here thinkin'," Nathan replied. "Thinkin' about bein' on top the Empire State Buildin', in New York City, with some water bombs, and leanin' out over the street when the people come out for lunch and ba-lam, man! Ba-laam!"

Eyes still closed, Nathan unclasped his hands and held one out, palm up.

"Gimme." Nathan hadn't heard that "please" was a magic word.

"Nathan, listen," Marco said.

"Listen nothin'," Nathan growled. "Gimme."

"Nathan, please! This is important!"

Nathan's outstretched hand went back to the other one over his stomach. They seemed to be petting it for a good job well done.

"Okay, Marco," he said. "I'll give you one minute. I'm rather pressed this mornin'."

Marco talked fast.

"Nathan, partner, I've got to have $7,000. I can't tell you why, but it's for a worthy cause. What I want to do is keep the money we earn from the route until I get the seven thousand. Then I'll turn all the proceeds over to you until you get your share. And then—and this is the good part, Nathan, the part you'll like—I'll turn over my entire pay to you for a

whole year, just to make up for your trouble. Can you beat a deal like that? What do you say, Nathan?"

Marco watched him. Nathan's eyes had never opened. His hands still clasped the favorite part of his body.

"What do you say, Nathan? Partner?"

"I say, 'Gimme.' " Slowly, sadly, eyes still shut, Nathan shook his head. "Look, man," he said. "I'm no pig—you more than anyone should know that. My wants are simple. A roof over my head, three meals a day with a few snacks, a little time to plan the future. But, Marco, I'm not in this business for my health."

His eye, his left eye, slid open like a lizard's and he used it to gaze at Marco. "We got a good thing goin' here, me an' you," he drawled. "Let's not destroy it. We got eighty papers —right?"

Marco said nothing about Mr. Perry dropping. It would just confuse matters at this point, and he could pick up a new customer with no trouble.

He could almost hear the adding maching clacking away in his partner's brain.

"Right," Nathan answered himself. "We get nine and three-fourths cents a week on every weekday paper—right? Right. And four and a half cents for each Sunday paper— right? Right. That gives us a weekly gross income of $11.40— right? Splittin' that down the middle, we each get $5.78 —right? Right. A nice tidy sum. Let's be satisfied with it."

"But what about my proposition?" Marco asked.

Nathan gave him a sad smile.

"Man, it would take you about twelve years just to get the seven grand. You'd be an old man of twenty-two, man, too shot to get square with me. No, Marco, we got a good thing goin' for us. Let's leave it alone."

Marco gritted his teeth.

Good ol' Perry was right. You could never get rich in the newspaper game. He counted out half the carrier's share of the route money and laid it in Nathan's outstretched palm. Then he turned and lurched out of the patio.

Behind him, Nathan lay in the hammock, hands over his stomach, eyes closed, a sweet smile on his face.

"Tell you what I'd really like, though," he was saying, "I'd get me one of them jets, one of them big two-hundred- seater jobs. Rip out the seats. Fill the whole ship with water bombs. Then come in over Canal Street on Mardi Gras at ten thousand feet . . . "

Marco walked along the narrow streets of the Quarter in

hot sunlight and then quick, cool shadow, without any idea of where he was walking or how long he walked, without even an idea that he was walking.

He bumped into people. People bumped into him. Cars passed, trucks, busses, hot-dog carts. A horse and buggy went by with a clop and a rattle. But Marco was aware of none of this.

What to do? What, oh, what to do?

He had no choice.

Coming to a drugstore, he slipped inside and went to the telephone booth. He dialed a number, then once more, covered the mouthpiece with his handkerchief.

"Audubon Park Zoo," a man answered.

He had a thin, high voice. It sounded as though he was in the monkey house. Either that or the monkeys were in *his* house.

"I don't suppose you could use a tiger," Marco said in his deepest voice.

"What?" the man asked. "Shut up there! Not you, sir," he added quickly. "Now, how's that again?"

"I would like to donate a healthy, well-mannered Royal Bengal tiger, male, to the zoo."

"A tiger, sir?" the man asked. "You'll have to see the director about that, and he's not here right now. I have no authority to accept donations of that size. Now if it was a zebra . . ."

"No," Marco conceded, "he isn't a zebra."

"Has he had his tetanus shot?"

"I don't know," Marco said miserably.

From the sounds that came over the telephone, there were at least two good-sized chimpanzees in the room, and one was tickling the other.

"How old is the animal?" the man asked.

"The *animal*," Marco snapped, "is about twenty years young."

"Too old." The man sighed. "Much too old. They have their own ideas at that age. Put a male and female in the same cage and all they do is fight, fight, fight. And as tigers get older, they take on a lean, drawn look. People say we're not feeding them, when actually we're feeding them more."

An earsplitting shriek came over the telephone . . . then what sounded like the two chimpanzees having a wrestling match.

"Wait!" the man yelled. "Put that down!"

A crash. A tinkle of glass. A dripping.

"Oh, no!" the man murmured. "Oh, my!"

"This tiger's in tiptop shape," Marco insisted. "Won't you reconsider?"

"Afraid not," the man said. "Oh, my, oh, my!"

"What am I going to do?" Marco asked.

"I'm sure I don't know, sir."

"If I don't do something right away," Marco cried, "some man's going to get a rifle and shoot him! Please, can't you make an exception in his case?"

"You'll have to see the director about that."

"Where is he?" Marco asked.

"You'll have to get that from the director when he comes back."

"When will he be back?"

"You'll have to get that from the director."

"Wait a minute," Marco said. "If I have to get it from him, what good will it do to find out when he's coming back when he's already back?"

"You'll have to—"

"I know," Marco said, "I'll have to get that from the director."

"Who is this calling, please?" the man asked.

"A friend."

"A friend of the *tiger?*"

"The best and only friend he's got," Marco said softly.

He hung up the receiver, which seemed to weigh fifty pounds, and his nickel went *clunk*. He felt so low he didn't even bother to check the coin-return box.

On the way out he had to go by the soda fountain. A man there was leaning down behind the counter. He wore a white short-sleeved jacket such as dentists use and a white cap with "Larry" stitched on it. Although he was leaning down, he towered over Marco. But then, Marco thought, who didn't? He was in a country of giants. And he had to play the game by their rules, even though he didn't know the rules and wasn't even sure about the game.

As Marco passed, Larry came up with a scoop of strawberry ice cream. He had a thick black mustache.

"Funny thing happened at work," Larry told his wife that night. "I'm making a strawberry milkshake—"

"That's a riot," his wife said.

"Wait," Larry said. "All of a sudden I look up. This kid with big ears and a skinned nose is staring at me with the biggest, brownest eyes you ever saw. His face gets white and he lets out a yell and bangs through the door and goes tearing up the street. He's probably still running."

10

HAM ON RYE

Marco ran until he could taste rusty nails. Then he kept on running. Up ahead, he saw the big stone and glass front of the New Orleans Public Library. He ran inside, as fugitives in olden days would run into a church with the cry of "Sanctuary!"

The N.O.P.L. reminded Marco of a church—a cathedral —cool and quiet, with the sunlight streaming through big windows, even though they didn't have stained glass in them.

He spent a lot of time in the library. He loved to stroll up and down the aisles with the thousands and thousands of books like walls on each side of him. Every single one of these books held a world of its own. It gave him a weird feeling to think that he could never, never read them all.

He was still puffing from his wild—and, he realized now, silly—flight. Already he was beginning to feel better. Marco was not exactly a scholar, but he had learned that, when he had a problem, it was best to find out something about it. When in doubt, look it up.

He looked up "The Lady or the Tiger?" in the card catalogue and found it in a volume of American short stories. He soon located the book and brought it to a table, where he carefully read the story. Then he snapped the book shut. No answers there. It was a fine story, written with a lot of style, right up to the end. Then it fell flat on its face.

He went to the encyclopedia, took out Volume 18, and carried it back to the table. It had good weight to it.

Opening to "Tiger," he ran his eye down the article—food—habits—good swimmers—climb trees. "Tigers," he read, "seem to be fond of haunting the neighborhood of old ruins."

Well, you couldn't haunt an older ruin than Perry's place at 420 Royal.

"They dwell chiefly in grassy plains or swamps."

Swamps! The word leaped out at him. New Orleans had nothing if it didn't have swamps. If worse came to worse . . .

"Hello, Marco."

"Hi, Miss Allen!"

"School work?"

"Not exactly."

"Had lunch?"

"No, ma'am."

"Come on."

Gaily she led the way between the walls of books to her book-lined office.

"I'm so glad to see you, Marco," she said, getting a package out of the filing cabinet. "I weakened again this morning and fixed too much. If you hadn't come along, I would have gone ahead and gobbled down the whole thing myself."

She giggled. Marco liked her giggle. He liked Miss Allen. She had a charming way of making you feel you were doing her a favor when it was really the other way around. She was a tall woman, with a pile of white hair, who was always trying to lose five pounds.

She and Marco sat across from each other at her desk. She spread out the lunch on the blotter.

"You take the ham," she said in her soft librarian's voice. "You don't have to worry about calories. I'll take the lettuce and tomato."

It was, Marco decided afterward, the best sandwich he had ever eaten: a thick, juicy, pink slice of ham on chewy rye bread, with mustard and dill pickle. (No butter—Miss Allen had not weakened *that* much.) So dark before, the future began to look brighter. It was, Marco thought, interesting to consider how many times the course of world history had been changed by two pieces of bread and a slice of ham.

The two friends topped off their meal at the fountain with a long, cold, non-caloric drink of good filtered Mississippi River water.

"Thank you. That was delicious," Marco said. There was, he decided, no point in telling Miss Allen his troubles. Not that he didn't trust her. He just didn't want to get her mixed up in them. For all her gay manner, she was bound to have troubles of her own.

Still, he couldn't help asking a question. "Miss Allen, how do you feel about tigers?"

"What do you mean, Marco?"

"Do you think the only good tiger is a dead tiger?"

Patting her pretty white pile of hair, Miss Allen gazed into space.

"I think," she said in her gentle voice, "that tigers are the most beautiful animals on this earth. We would be much the poorer without them. Oh, I know they're sinister and cruel, according to our way of thinking. But I'm sure they think we're just as sinister and just as cruel. It all depends upon your point of view."

"Well, thanks again and 'bye."

"Good-by, Marco." Miss Allen watched him with a wondering smile until he disappeared behind a thousand books.

Back on the street, Marco squared his shoulders. So he needed seven thousand bucks. So what? He already had the Chief's $5 and his $5.70 from the paper route. Leaving out the 70 cents for emergencies, he had $10. All in the world he had to do was collect $6,990 somewhere.

Now he was marching again and humming his marching song. Sure he had a problem. But he would lick it. He was eleven!

As he went stepping along, the words to the song came to him. He sang them to himself.

"THE TIGER MARCH"

Blow the bugles, roll the drums (drums, drums)
Here he comes (comes, comes)
Down the street with a most unusual beat—
Tiger! Yay, Tiger!
It's hup, two, three—not four
With Tiger!

Oh, he's striped orange and black,
With white teeth in his jaws
And sharp claws in his paws.
But you can take it from me,
He only walks on three—
'Cause he's Tiger!

So it's hup, two, three—not four
With Tiger! TIGER!

As Marco was coming up Pirate's Alley, the clock in the belfry of St. Louis Cathedral struck one. The alley was loaded with rain puddles. Marco thought seriously about stomping in them but let it go. Pompous, purple pigeons were strutting around as if they owned the place. But, don't worry, they got out of his way fast enough when Marco Fennerty, Junior came swinging along in one-two time.

Across Chartres Street, in Jackson Square, a cardinal (maybe *the* cardinal) was singing a new tune.

"Cheer! Cheer! Cheer!"

The artists, wearing their beards, berets, and sandals, were out in force. Their paintings were hung along the iron picket fence for the crowd of tourists to see and, hopefully, buy. Children sported around the iron benches, where old men sat playing checkers.

In the middle of the square, the bronze statue of Andrew

Jackson sat proudly on his rearing horse, doffing his hat. Marco snapped Old Hickory a salute, marching past on his way toward the invisible Mississippi.

All along the water front, blocking out the river, stretched the gray steel warehouses. Marco kept going until he found one open, then slipped inside. It was huge and dark. The headlights of trucks working there were like yellow eyes in the gloom. It made Marco think of a robber cave, stuffed with boxes and bales and sacks and crates—cargo for and from all over the world.

Then a cool breeze swatted him in the face.

Rounding a tall pile of smelly cowhides, he saw the bright glare of an open doorway. Beyond it, like a picture in a frame, a little red tugboat was charging up the wide brown river.

Marco walked along the busy wharf, dodging fork-lift trucks and the swinging cargo nets of the ships as they loaded and unloaded. The big, tough Mississippi hurried past, showing its sinews.

Down the river, down the Gulf of Mexico, across the Atlantic and the Mediterranean, through the Suez Canal, down the Red Sea, around the Indian Ocean . . . and Tiger would be home. (Home!)

Coming to a big freighter, he stopped and studied her decks. As far as he could see, not a soul was aboard. Swiftly he climbed up the swaying gangplank.

Now if he could do it, in broad daylight, surely Tiger, under cover of night . . .

"Hey, you!"

A man popped out of a dark passageway. He wore a cap and a gray uniform with a badge on his chest. He had a gun on his hip and a frown on his wrinkled, raw face.

Marco gave him a bright smile, as if delighted to see him.

The frown deepened to a scowl. The man had a face like seven pounds of uncooked liver.

"Just what d'you think you're doing on this here vessel?"

"Visiting," Marco said. "You know—visiting."

"Nobody gets on this here vessel without a pass. You got a pass?"

Marco patted all his pockets twice.

"Not this time," he said, still smiling.

"Off!"

Marco went down the swaying gangplank. At the bottom, he turned to wave good-by.

"Don't come back!" the man yelled.

Marco sat on a coil of rope with his chin in his hands, staring at the bustling river. A tugboat was taking a tanker upstream. Another tugboat was pushing a barge downstream. On the Algiers side of the river the Canal Street ferry gave a toot, which was answered with a toot-toot by the ferry on the New Orleans side. Then, as in a traffic jam when one driver starts the others honking, all the ships in port started to blast away on their horns.

It was good that they all seemed to be having fun.

"What's wrong, kid?"

Marco looked up.

The first thing he saw was the tattoo. A blue snake went around and around the man's brown forearm. He had his sleeves rolled up and was carrying his coat over one shoulder. He was very tanned. His blond hair and eyebrows were bleached almost white by the sun.

He grinned down at Marco.

"Are you a seaman?" Marco asked.

"Right you are, sir," the man answered, saluting. "Sandy

Fairfax reporting. Best A.B. this side of Suez—though I must admit I'm a bit the worse for wear at the moment, after a round of visits with friends ashore."

Marco gazed up at him. "Do you have a ship?"

" 'Do I have a ship?' he asks. 'Of course I have a ship,' says I. What A.B. worthy of the name doesn't have a ship? There she lies, bless her rusty bottom, the *Congo Trader*."

Looking up the wharf to where Sandy pointed, Marco saw a huge black-and-white freighter. She was taking on farm machinery. As he watched, a big yellow tractor rose up, swinging like a pendulum at the end of the steel cables, then went clunk inside the ship.

"We sail tonight for Calcutta," Sandy said.

"Calcutta!"

"Aye, mate, Calcutta. And other ports of call along the way. Wanna come with us?"

"I can't," Marco said. "But I have a very good friend who can."

"Any friend of a friend is a friend of Sandy Fairfax, A.B." Squatting down on his heels, the tattooed man heard Marco's story through. "No problem," he said with a happy-go-lucky twirl of his hand. "You bring this lion or whatever it is down to the ship at seven-thirty tonight and we'll take it with us. No problem."

"Honest?" If he hadn't been eleven, Marco would have clapped his hands for joy. "But what about the charge?" he asked. "I don't have too much money."

"No problem," Sandy repeated. "Leave it to me."

Then Marco thought of something. "Sure it will be okay with the skipper?"

"No problem," Sandy said again. "The Old Man owes me a favor. I saved him from bloodthirsty headhunters in the Solomons, or sharks in the Java Sea. Something like that."

The Old Man. How nice, Marco thought, for your father to be captain of your ship.

He kept talking to Sandy, arranging such details as meals and sleeping quarters and having the tiger swim ashore to the jungle as the *Congo Trader* drew close to Calcutta. Sandy kept nodding his head and saying, "No problem."

"I'd better get going, Sandy," Marco said at last. "Got a mess of things to do. See you at seven-thirty."

"No problem," Sandy said and raised his hand in a farewell salute.

11

UNDER THE BED SHEET

When Marco got home from throwing papers, he found a note on the kitchen table, propped up against the bowl of oatmeal.

Dear Marco:
Supper on kitchen table. Won't be home till late.
Regards,
Ophelia Drack

There was something funny about that note. Not the *Ophelia* (although that was pretty funny) but the *Dear Marco* business mainly. Right now, however, he hadn't time to think about it.

Going into his bedroom, Marco pulled a sheet off his bed and held it up. Too small. Much too small. He checked his father's bed. One sheet had a big rip. The other was in tatters.

He went into Mrs. Drack's room, folded down her bedspread, and pulled off a sheet. It was so new it crackled. He tucked it under his arm and left for 420 Royal.

Strange noises were coming from the tiger's quarters as Marco walked up the carriageway. There was a dribbling sound, then a rumble and a tumble and a crash. Marco ran across the courtyard.

"Tiger?" he called. "Are you all right?"

He threw open the door. The ball came bouncing out, Tiger right behind it.

"Oh!" Marco cried, pleased and relieved at the same time. "You were playing with your ball!"

The tiger was delighted to see him. Marco watched as he swatted the ball with his paw, then chased it, bouncing, around the courtyard.

"Good news, Tiger," he said. "I've arranged passage for you on a ship that leaves tonight for Calcutta!"

Tiger usually had a bored expression, even when he wasn't bored. But now both furry white eyebrows shot up as if to say, "You're kidding."

"I'm serious," Marco insisted. "We'll hole up at my place till dark. Then we'll scoot down to the ship just before she sails. I'll fill you in on all the details later, but now let's get this sheet on you so we can pass through the city unnoticed."

Tiger gave him a look but let Marco drape the sheet over him. Then, opening the front door, Marco peered up and down Royal Street. When the coast was clear, he beckoned Tiger to come on.

Tiger came on, rather sheepishly, like a dog that has just had a bath. It was obvious that he looked upon this as a mess of boyish nonsense, but he was going to be a good sport. His nose stuck out of one end of the sheet, and his tail out of the other. Still and all, no one seeing him could be absolutely sure he was a tiger.

In the French Quarter of New Orleans, there are ways of getting from one spot to another without staying on the main streets. Marco led Tiger down shadowy alleyways, over crumbling brick walls, across empty, echoing courtyards, and through deserted buildings, where they left a trail of footprints and paw prints behind them in the thick dust.

He slammed on the brakes, stared at whatever it was under the sheet, shook his head violently, and roared on . . .

Once, when they had to cross a side street, a man in a little beanie cap came roaring along in a red sports car. He slammed on the brakes, stared at whatever it was under the sheet, shook his head violently, and roared on, honking his horn for all it was worth.

Marco peeked around the corner of his block. The street was empty. Then a tap-tap-tap sounded behind him. The Chief! There was nothing for Marco to do but say hello. The three of them walked along together.

"What's that with you, Marco?" the Chief asked.

"The tiger."

"Oh!" The Chief smiled. "Anyway, he's a big devil, all right. Did he hurt his paw?"

"No, sir. He always walks on three."

"Well, I'll say one thing for him, Marco. He sure *smells* like a tiger."

Up in the apartment, free of the bed sheet, Tiger wandered from room to room, rubbing against this, sniffing that. Then he turned to Marco with a look that said, "S-a-a-a-a-y, this is *all right!*"

It was nice, Marco thought, to have a tiger in the house.

He fixed his guest a bowl of oatmeal. When he had polished it off, Marco sang him "The Tiger March." It made quite a hit. Marco sang it all the way through again. He only wished good ol' Perry could be there to hear it.

Then Marco sat Tiger down in the living room and told him about his day, leaving out only the part about the man with the mustache. When Marco got to Sandy Fairfax, a change came over Tiger.

So excited and happy before, now he acted bored. As Marco talked, Tiger kept shaking his great head from side to side and giving low, coughing growls that seemed to say, "You couldn't!" and "You didn't really!" and "Oh, no!" It was clear he did not think much of Marco's seaman friend. He was not even impressed with the snake tattoo.

Could he be jealous? Marco wondered. Jealous of a *tattoo?*

When Marco had finished, Tiger gave him a long look. Then he groaned and lay down with a crash that shook the apartment. At once, the telephone rang.

"Marco, are you jumping up there?" the lady downstairs demanded.

"Sorry, Mrs. Zumbo." He gave Tiger a look. "It won't happen again."

Tiger lay with his head on one paw, breathing deeply, twitching his ears, watching Marco.

"You don't think it's going to work," Marco said.

Tiger stretched his neck. *No!*

"You're a pessimist," the boy remarked. "You always look on the gloomy side of things."

No, Tiger told him in a series of neck stretchings, eyebrow cockings, tail whappings, right ear twitchings, and left whisker quiverings. He was not a pessimist. He was a realist. He had learned from long experience that wishing did not make it so. A guy had to be practical.

Something else he had learned: You don't trust a tattooed man.

"You'll see," Marco insisted. "Sandy's a real nice fella. Everything's going to work out, and I'll tell you why. I'm gonna *make* it work out. I'm eleven!"

Tiger lay there breathing hard, twitching his ears, and watching Marco with his big, golden eyes that blinked, blinked in the gathering darkness. . . .

Then it was time. Marco jumped up.

"Okay, Tiger, this is it." He covered his friend with Mrs. Drack's bed sheet.

As they were crossing the railroad tracks to get to the water front, a boat horn gave a long, hoarse blast. Marco and Tiger started to walk faster. By the time they came through the warehouse onto the wharf, they were running.

Far down the dark wharf, a ship, all lighted up, was unloading bananas. But the space that the *Congo Trader* had been in that afternoon was empty! She was backing out into the river.

"Hey!" Marco yelled. "Wait!"

He ran down the wharf, shouting, Tiger behind him, bed sheet popping in the breeze. They came to a flight of stone steps that led down to a little dock. A rowboat was chained to an iron post there.

Marco ran down the steps. If only it wasn't locked!

It wasn't.

If only it had oars!

It did, on the bottom of the boat.

Marco jumped in and slipped the oars into the oarlocks. Tiger sat in the stern, which shot down with his weight. Marco shoved off with an oar and began to row across and down the swift, black river.

Behind him, the *Congo Trader* gave another blast on her horn. She was heading upstream to turn around.

"We'll cut her off, Tiger, never fear," Marco assured him, pulling at the oars with all his eleven years' strength. "Don't worry. Everything's—going to work out okay. AHOY, *CONGO TRADER!* It's just—like everything else. If you want it badly enough—you'll get it. But you've got—to work. You've got to—put your back into it. *CONGO TRADER,* AHOY!"

He glanced over his shoulder.

The freighter had completed her turn and now was coming down the river toward them, the bow wave a white mus-

tache under the black nose. She was making good speed—
very good speed indeed.

Marco fell back with a jolt.

The port oar had jumped out of its lock. Slipping it back
into place took precious seconds.

"These things—will happen to oarsmen—who lack the
proper—experience, Tiger," Marco gasped. "But don't worry.
AHOY, *CONGO TRADER!* Taking it up—to thirty-six,
Tiger. Stroke! Stroke! Stroke! SHIP AHOY!"

Tiger watched the boy with his golden eyes.

Beyond him, Marco could see St. Louis Cathedral and

the glow of lights from Jackson Square. He felt hot blisters forming on his palms. His arms were getting stiff. So was his back.

When he looked over his shoulder, he could see the whole freighter, stem to stern. "Ahoy!"

Then the stupid port oar jumped out of its lock again. Tiger watched with his glowing eyes as Marco fought to get it back into place. His hands weren't working too well. The blisters had broken and the palms were raw.

From behind him came the churning of the propeller. Marco knew without looking that the *Congo Trader* had already passed them.

He put everything he had into his arms and back. But what he had wasn't so much any more. Behind him, the *clutter-clutter* of the propeller was getting softer, softer.

"Ahoy!" The call was much fainter than before.

Then they started to roll. They had hit the freighter's wake. It made the rowing all the harder. Marco kept on rowing, though. To himself he sang "The Tiger March."

And then, and *then* the propeller noise got louder.

Marco didn't dare turn around. . . . Finally he did. The *Congo Trader* had reversed engines. She was laying to.

Ah, yes, they had come to Algiers Point. On the far bank of the river, the Esplanade Street traffic light was shining red. And around the sharp bend was coming a great, big, beautiful tanker.

"See?" Marco told Tiger. "What did I tell you?"

He rowed up to the side of the *Congo Trader*. The monstrous ship hung over them like a black cliff. He shouted up to the bridge, "Ahoy, *Congo Trader!*"

"All right, all right," a voice called down. "What's all the excitement?" The voice was gruff, with an Irish lilt to it.

"I've got to see Sandy Fairfax, A.B.!" Marco yelled. His hands were sore. His back felt broken in two.

"Sandy Fairfax, A.B., is it?" the voice demanded. "Get along with you!"

"Where is he, please?" Marco called. "It's of the utmost importance!"

"Where is he now? And where else would he be when there's work to be done? Dead to the world in his bunk, of course, the tattooed bum!"

Down the river, the tanker was coming along fast, a tough little tugboat on either side of her.

"Oh, please!" Marco shouted. "Can I speak to his father then?"

"His father! Indeed, I wouldn't be knowing where in this wide world to find that unhappy soul."

"He's captain of the ship!" Marco yelled. "Sandy said he was his Old Man!"

The tanker passed. The light was green.

"Look," the Irishman said. "I'm master of the *Congo Trader*. And Sandy Fairfax is no son of mine, thank the good Lord. On a ship, the captain is always called the Old Man." He added—not so gruffly, "There's a lot you've got to learn, bucko."

"Yessir," Marco answered meekly. "But I have something for Sandy."

"Let's haul it aboard then," the captain urged. "I've got a schedule to meet."

On the bridge, a powerful searchlight snapped on and swung out and down, a long yellow finger poking through the river mist.

"Thought so," the captain mused. "Laundry. Sandy does always be leaving his laundry in every port. If it wasn't for me—Saints preserve us, a tiger!"

The bed sheet had fallen off Tiger's head as he gazed up at the bridge, blinking in the light.

"Please, sir," Marco called. "Sandy promised to take him back to India for me!"

"Of course," the captain said. "Sandy would promise anything to anybody when he's had a busy shore leave—and mean every word of it. But let's be practical, bucko. I can't be taking that thing back to India. Every man aboard would jump ship. And I couldn't just turn it loose there. India has her quarantine regulations and all, just like we do. You wouldn't be wanting me to break the law, would you?"

"No, sir," Marco answered. "I hadn't thought of that."

"I'm sorry, bucko," the captain said. "And don't be too hard on Sandy. He's a good lad all in all. Good-by to you, bucko, and good luck."

"Good-by, sir."

Marco and Tiger sat in the rowboat, rocking in the wake of the *Congo Trader* as she went churning down the river at slow bell. They watched until her running lights disappeared around the bend. Then Marco, avoiding Tiger's eyes, started the long, hard pull back to the dock.

12

THE FIGHT

Slowly they walked back to 420 Royal, two sad, sad figures, one of them partly covered with a bed sheet. Neither was in the mood for exchanging ideas. But when Marco had closed the front door behind them, he turned to Tiger.

"Go on," he cried. "Say it. Say, 'I told you so'!"

Tiger made no sign at all that Marco could see. Only his sad gold eyes glowed, blinking in the darkness.

"Tell me I'm not practical," Marco went on. "Tell me I've got a lot to learn."

Tiger just watched him.

"Careful, Tiger," Marco warned. "Let's not say anything we'll be sorry for later." He had such a big lump in his throat that it was hard to talk.

Tiger just watched him.

"Okay," Marco said. "Maybe I *have* messed this up. Maybe I have. But I tried. I did my best. I did my very best!"

Tiger blinked.

"All right," Marco demanded. "You're so smart. What do *you* think we ought to do."

Whap! Whap! Whap! The tail beat on the flagstones as Tiger signaled, "I don't know."

"Sure," Marco said. "It's easy enough for other people to

find fault when they're just standing on the side lines. But let me tell you something now. I'll take the man out there on the field who's giving it all he's got, win or lose—any day!"

The yellow eyes went out, then came back on.

"Well, say it," Marco insisted. "I'm a silly little boy with silly little dreams—is that it?"

Tiger groaned.

"I don't have to stand here and be insulted by a stupid old tiger!" Marco yelled.

He stalked off, slamming the front door behind him.

Marco could not remember when he had not run up the stairs to his apartment. Tonight, he almost crawled. He was *some* tired. He had never been so utterly tired, so miserable. He wanted to go to bed and sleep, sleep, sleep. Maybe tomorrow would be better. It had to be. He couldn't possibly mess up another day as badly as this.

He unlocked the door and stumbled into the apartment. The lights were on.

He tried to remember if he had left them burning when he and Tiger had gone to the water front. He couldn't remember. He couldn't think. He went to his room and shut the door. He was too tired to take off his clothes. He sat down on the bed. The springs groaned and so did he.

Heavy, angry footsteps sounded outside the door. Marco took a deep breath. The knob turned. The door flew open with a bang. Mrs. Drack stood there. She seemed to fill the doorway.

"Hi, Mrs. Drack," Marco said. "Pardon me for not getting up. I thought you weren't coming home till late."

"Yes, I'm sure you did," she snarled. "Exactly what are you trying to pull here, Marco?"

"I don't exactly know what you have reference to, Mrs. Drack." So! he thought. She had set a trap for him.

"I'll tell you what I mean. Where have you been?"

"Out, Mrs. Drack."

"Out where?"

"Just out, Mrs. Drack," Marco said. "We'll talk in the morning, okay? I'm beat."

"We'll talk now! What are you trying to get away with? What do you mean by sneaking into my room and tearing up my bed? Where's my bed sheet?"

"Bed sheet, Mrs. Drack?" Then and only then did Marco remember that he had left the sheet at 420 Royal.

"Bed sheet! Bed sheet! Bed sheet! Your father's going to hear about this. He paid good money for that sheet. You'd better get it back in A-One condition or there's going to be war. You can take if from me."

But you can take it from me,
He only walks on three . . .

Oh, Tiger! Tiger!

Mrs. Drack went stomping up and down the room, talking of war, waving her long scarecrow arms, shaking a bony finger in his face—now and then jerking his ear to get his attention. But Marco was too miserable to mind.

Then there came a soft knock at the front door.

13

THE BOY FROM NIGER

"I just hope it's your father, that's all," Mrs. Drack said through her teeth. She went to the door, opened it and screamed.

"*Eeee-YAK!*"

Tiger was in the doorway, sitting up, with his front paws hanging before him. In his teeth, neatly rolled, was Mrs. Drack's bed sheet.

She did not bother to thank him.

"Tiger!" she cried, running into her room. "Tiger!" she shouted, running out with her purse. "Tiger!" she screamed, clamping on her silly little hat. "Tiger!" she shrieked, crashilating down the back stairs. "Help, police, a tiger!"

That was the last of Mrs. Drack. (Later, when she had read in the papers what had happened to Tiger, she telephoned Marco's father long distance from Baton Rouge, Louisiana, offering to come back. But he told her no thank you. He had already hired another housekeeper—a little woman with a sweet disposition, gray hair, and brown freckles, who cooked Marco ham and eggs, and steak, and all kinds of stuff, but never oatmeal.)

Marco reached up and took the bed sheet out of Tiger's mouth.

"Hi, Tiger!" he said.

"Ho!" the tiger answered. "Ha!"

He rubbed his silky throat against Marco's cheek.

At first Marco was going to accept Tiger's apology and let it go at that. But then he took his friend's right paw in both hands and said, "You were right, Tiger. About everything. And I'm sorry for all the things I said. I want to be friends."

They shook on it.

"We don't have much time," the boy remarked. "Were you followed?"

Glancing over his shoulder, Tiger whapped his tail on the floor. *I don't know.*

"Let's get out of here," Marco urged.

They started down the front stairs. They had almost reached the first floor when a prowl car pulled up outside with the red signal light flashing, and two policemen jumped out. Marco and the tiger ran back up to the apartment. Marco locked and bolted the front door. Between them, he and Tiger pushed a heavy chest of drawers against the door. Then they slipped out the back way.

From all over New Orleans came the cry of police sirens. Marco and Tiger were running across the patio to the gate when two prowl cars pulled up on the street outside. In seconds, two more came screaming up. Then the motorcycle policemen came, a whole roaring company of them.

More prowl cars arrived upon the scene, along with cars filled with newspaper and television reporters and cameramen. Mounted police came galloping down the street like a cavalry charge, the horses' hoofs clopping on the pavement. From the sound of things, Marco guessed that his father must be the only officer minding the police station. A fire truck came thundering up and, last of all, a garbage truck. The driver had come along just for kicks.

The night was deafening with the shouts, the slamming of doors, and the roar of the motorcycles, whose riders kept gunning the motors in their excitement.

Mrs. Zumbo stuck her head out of the window.

"Stop that humbug or I'll call the police!"

In the street, powerful floodlights came on. Gungah! Marco and Tiger crouched in the deep shadow behind the patio wall. There was no place to hide.

"Quiet!" someone yelled.

"Quiet!" yelled someone else.

All was quiet, except for the distant pounding on the front door of Marco's apartment. The policemen would be through that door before long.

In the street, Police Chief Kelley glanced at the cameramen and straightened his tie. Then, picking up a bull horn, he blew into it and said, "Testing, testing. One, two, three. Can you hear me in there?"

Marco and Tiger, crouching in the shadow, kept their silence.

"This is Chief of Police Kelley, K-E-L-L-E-Y," the Chief said, glancing at the reporters. "We've got you surrounded. You don't have a chance. Come out with your hands up, er"—another policeman whispered into his ear—"Make that with hands up and paws down, y'hear?"

Marco and Tiger stuck in their boots.

On the street, a policeman came up to Chief Kelley with a tear-gas gun.

"Guess I better give 'em a whiff of this," he said.

"Just a minute, Patrolman Snowman," the Chief ordered

"Corporal Ginsberg got to do it last time!" Patrolman Snowman reminded him. "Now it's my turn!"

"I'm going to count ten," Chief Kelley said into the bull horn. "One . . . two . . ."

Pop! The tear-gas shell shot out of the gun, hit the patio wall, and fell back into the street. A thick gray cloud came hissing out.

"Who's (cough) the idiot who fired (cough) that tear gas?" Chief Kelley demanded.

"Corporal Ginsberg," Patrolman Snowman told him, coughing . . . and fired a second shell. This was aimed a little better, but it didn't quite clear the wall. It, too, fell back into the street, hissing like a dragon.

The night was muggy; no breeze. The gray cloud got thicker, ever thicker, spreading out until all the policemen and firemen and newspapermen and television men and the garbage man and Mrs. Zumbo and even the police horses were coughing and snorting, with fat tears rolling down their noses.

Inside the patio, Marco and Tiger could see none of this —but they could hear. Upstairs, the police officers had forced the door open and were running through the apartment.

"Quick, Tiger!" Marco whispered. "It's our only chance. Over the wall with you. I'll meet you on the corner."

Tiger bunched together and leaped up on top of the wall and vanished in three easy movements. Marco turned on a garden hose in the patio and soaked his handkerchief. Then, taking a deep breath and spreading the handkerchief over his face, he went through the gate just as the two policemen came banging down the back stairs.

Marco felt his way along the rough brick wall, keeping his eyes shut and trying not to breathe. But the tear gas got through to him, stinging his eyes and nose something fierce.

Blindly, Marco stumbled toward the corner. He was out of the tear-gas cloud, but his eyes and nose still burned. Suddenly, he realized he had not told Tiger which corner. Panic seized him.

Wiping his eyes, he *made* them see.

There was a street lamp on the corner, shining down on the empty, black asphalt. Word had spread fast and people were inside their homes, windows down, doors locked. Behind him, the crowd of police and firemen and all were still stumbling around in the tear gas, bumping into each other and crying as if their poor hearts would break.

"Ho!" Tiger said from a doorway.

Keeping off the main thoroughfares and in the shadows as much as possible, Marco and Tiger worked their way down to Lower Canal Street. This was a dark and lonely place at night where the empty trolleys used to turn around—when there were trolleys on Canal Street.

Slipping across the broad pavement, they stole past the silent buildings and still trucks of the warehouse district. The bright lights of St. Charles Street shone through the magnolias of Lafayette Square.

Marco had Tiger wait around the corner until a streetcar came along with a rumble and a clatter, as proud and grand as a Carnival float. The rear doors flew open and the steps banged down. Marco and Tiger climbed aboard, the conductor jumping off as soon as he saw the tiger.

Climbing up on the stool, Marco rang the bell three times—once for himself, twice for Tiger. Up front, the motorman—invisible behind a black curtain—pushed the throttle forward.

There was a jerk, then a growl, turning to a whine, and the St. Charles streetcar was on its rocking, swaying passage through the night to uptown New Orleans. Beyond lay the levee. Beyond that the swamp.

Marco sat in the back of the car. Tiger lay beside him on the floor.

Slowly, painfully they went grinding around Lee Circle.
High above them the statue of General Robert E. Lee, a man
who had his problems too, stood on its stone lookout post,
facing forever north.

Now the streetcar started to pick up speed.

So far, so good—so far and so good, the wheels seemed
to say.

They were really clicking along now. The only other
passenger was a very large man in the front seat who was
making walrus noises in his sleep. He woke himself with a
snort and got off at Jackson Avenue.

So far, so good—so far and so good.

The rails were laid over grass now. The streetcar was
rushing past trees that were so close you could reach out and
touch them.

"Here's the plan, Tiger," Marco explained. "We'll ride to
St. Charles and Carrollton. Then we'll get off and climb up on
the levee. Then we'll walk along the levee till we come to the
swamp. After that, you're on your own."

He reached down and slapped the tiger on the shoulder.

"You'll think you're back in India, Tiger!"

Tiger looked up at him with his sad eyes.

"We can't do anything else," Marco said. "If you stick
around here, you're as good as dead. I'm not worried about
the police. They only do their duty and won't fire unless they
have to. But some crazy guy with a mustache is going to
shoot you down, just for the fun of it!"

Tiger nodded, or maybe his head just bobbed in the
bouncing car.

"At least in the swamp you'll have a chance," Marco
pointed out. "And you can watch the sun come up and go
down and you can sleep under the stars, just like in India!"

Yes. Tiger cocked a sad eyebrow. Then he laid his head on a paw.

They went rocking along. At Napoleon, a small crowd was waiting. The people in front got on, saw the tiger and got off, pushing the others back. It happened so fast Marco couldn't count them. He rang the bell five times, then gave it one to grow on.

The streetcar jumped ahead. Looking back, Marco saw one of the people run into a telephone booth.

"We're almost there, Tiger!" he cried.

Tiger said nothing. He did not look up·

Marco scratched him behind the ears. He read the chewing-gum and razor-blade ads and the signs. "In the interest of safety, please do not talk to driver while car is in motion." "NO SMOKING."

Now they were rumbling past the big stone houses of the rich people. And now the wheels had a different message.

You're doing it wrong, you're doing it wrong, a-wrong, a-wrong.

They were just passing Henry Clay Street when the first squad car tore by, heading uptown, siren screaming, signal light flashing red arrows. Two more followed close behind, along with a couple of motorcycle policemen. Then came a pickup truck filled with men in sports clothes and overalls. They all held rifles or shotguns. Marco spotted one man with a mustache.

Through the front window, he saw that the police were setting up a roadblock ahead. He pulled the buzzer.

"Come on, Tiger!"

The streetcar screeched to a stop. Marco and Tiger jumped off the back way.

"Charlie?" the motorman called, laughing. "You'll call

me crazy but I could swear I just saw a tiger get off. *Charlie?"*

On the lake side of the street, like forts or castles or something, stood the huge, grim buildings of Tulane University. On the river side was the dark forest of Audubon Park.

Marco and Tiger ran for the trees of the park. Marco kept waiting for the buzz of bullets and the crack of rifles. But none came, and they made the trees okay. They had gone only a little way into the park, however, before Marco fell. He knew he could go no farther.

"Go on, Tiger," he gasped. "I'll try to stall them. I don't know, maybe you can make the swamp from here."

Tiger gave a quick, coughing growl that sounded like "No!" He crouched down. Marco climbed aboard, too tired to argue, too tired to care where they were going, but not too tired to smile as he rode on the tiger.

Behind them came the sad, the terrible wail of sirens.

They went up the bridle path. Moonlight coming down through the trees glowed on the black earth like puddles of spilled milk. The tiger ran with a lumpy motion that was somewhat like a gallop and somewhat like a trot. Anyway, it was getting them there—wherever that was.

They were running alongside the lagoon, all silver and black in the moonlight. A couple of ducks, or maybe swans, watched them solemnly from the water. They passed the stone bridge leading to the golf course. From out of the dark ahead came the blast of a boat horn.

Then they saw the long blue glow of Magazine Street. They crossed the wide, empty roadway and plunged into the bushes and trees on the far side. The wailing sirens behind them were closer. There came another mournful sound but Marco didn't know what it was. Tiger snarled. He knew.

There was a rolling jolt as he shifted from one foot to the other, and they were off again at greater speed, past the dark merry-go-round, past the covered rides of the amusement park. But the sirens seemed to be gaining, along with that other sound. Sometimes, through the trees, Marco could see the red flashes of the signal lights.

The tiger stopped, so suddenly that Marco almost shot over his head. Looking up, he saw the big iron gate of Audubon Park Zoo, gleaming in the moonlight.

Stiffly he climbed off the tiger's back. His legs felt so

funny he almost fell. He went up to the gate and put his hand on the knob.

"Please," he whispered.

The knob turned easily, but the gate didn't move. It was locked tight.

The sirens were loud, getting louder. They seemed to be coming from all directions. The tiger snarled. Now Marco knew what that other sound was.

Dogs! The men had hunting dogs with them.

Though the bushes and through the trees, flashlights were flickering like fireflies. Sometimes you could hear the shouts of the eager men. The bars of the gate were hard and cold against Marco's back.

He turned around and hammered on the gate with his fists.

"Sanctuary!" he shouted. "Let us in!"

Deep inside the gloom of the zoo, he could see what looked like a toy house. The roof gleamed like cake frosting in the moonlight. A dim light was burning in the window. It had the look of a light left on all night.

The fence around the zoo was high—too high—and, besides, it was topped with a cruel tangle of barbed wire. Maybe in his younger days Tiger could—No, not even then.

Behind them, the yowling and the shouts were getting louder. Marco tried to ignore them.

"Hey!" he yelled. "Let us in!"

The door to the house opened and a thin little man appeared in the doorway. With the light behind him, he looked as though he had been cut out of black cardboard.

"The zoo doesn't open till nine o'clock in the morning," the man called. "The animals are all asleep. Have a little consideration."

Marco recognized the thin, high voice.

"I'm Marco Fennerty, Junior!" he yelled. "The friend of the tiger. I talked to you on the telephone this morning!"

"Kindly keep your voice down," the man called. "It's taken me this long to get the baby elephant to sleep, and I'm not about to have him waked up!"

"You've got to let us in!"

The man came up to the gate, moving into the moonlight. He was good and mad.

"Look, I can't tell you any more than I told you before," he said in his thin, high voice. "You'll have to see the director —and he's in Chicago. I don't have no authority! Now take that tiger of yours and get out of here!"

"But they'll kill him!" Marco cried. "See them coming? Hear them yell? They'll be here in a minute. They'll shoot him down like nothing!"

The man paused. Then he shook his head. It looked silver in the moonlight.

"I'm sorry, kid. I really am. But you don't understand. It's easy enough for you. You're young, full of hops and vinegar. But, believe me, I can't take it upon myself. I did it once. Accepted a gorilla. And what does he do, first crack off the bat? Busts the mayor—on the nozzle, mind you, on the nozzle!"

The man shook his silvery head again.

"Anything up to a zebra, yes. Beyond that, I'm telling you, the director would have my hide."

"Call him!" Marco cried. "Here, this will pay for it." He held out his ten dollars.

"Call him at *this* hour?" the man demanded. "You *do* want me to get skinned alive, don't you?"

"All right then," Marco said. "Wait till the morning. But at least put the tiger up overnight."

"Anyway," the man pointed out, "we don't have an empty cage."

There was no ignoring the pursuing men now, nor the hounds—they were that close.

"Put him in with another tiger!" Marco yelled.

"Can't," the man sighed. "Cages are all filled. 'Cept for Norah Sue's. And she's so mean and hateful nobody can put up with her."

"Try it!" Marco yelled.

"Try it! Man, we tried it—not once but twice. Norah Sue like to tear them poor tigers to shreds. It gets right expensive after a while."

Marco pushed his face through the bars.

"Listen," he said earnestly. "You're looking at a famous tiger here. Take it from me, a veteran newspaperman. His story will be in every paper in the country. People will come from all over just to look at him and say they saw him. And to kids like me, he'll be a hero!"

He glanced down at Tiger. He was paying no attention. He was crouched, fangs bared, claws out, waiting quietly for the dogs and the men—and death.

If only, Marco thought, if only the police can get here first. It didn't sound like they would, though. He turned back to the man behind the bars.

The man looked at Marco and slowly shook his head.

"Sorry, kid."

"Please!"

The man looked at Marco some more . . . and looked at the tiger . . . and looked at Marco.

"Well, here goes nothing," he said, taking the money. He unlocked the gate. "Come on, boy."

Tiger went in and the gate clanged shut. Marco stood

outside as Tiger trotted behind the man into the moonlight and the darkness of the zoo.

"Good-by, Tiger!" he called.

Tiger gave him a happy roar.

"You must understand," the man said, turning around. "I can't guarantee nothing. It's up to the director entirely."

"I understand," Marco answered. "Good-by, Tiger!"

Tiger gave him a second happy roar.

Marco stood at the gate as the men and dogs came bounding up, wild-eyed and snarling. It was hard to say which, dogs or men, were more disappointed—or madder at Marco for defeating them. Marco pressed back against the gate as they closed in on him.

That was when the police arrived, along with a couple of newspapermen. Marco granted a brief press conference, then accepted a ride home in a prowl car. In his honor, the officers kept the siren going the whole way. It sure was a nice, joyful sound.

14

A WALK THROUGH THE PARK

The story was on page one Sunday morning, along with a big photograph of Tiger and a smaller one of Marco. Of the two, Marco had to admit, Tiger took the better picture. The boy sat down on the curb by the substation and read the whole story through in the gray early-morning light before he delivered his papers.

Big black headlines announced:

TIGER SPREADS TERROR
THROUGH NEW ORLEANS

Boy and Jungle Cat
Lead Cops Wild Chase

The story was well written and accurate—as far as it went. Fennerty was spelled right (and so was Kelley). The story told most of what had happened Saturday night, starting with the commotion at Marco's apartment house, going through the ride on the St. Charles streetcar, and ending with all the humbug at the zoo. Tiger was quite a hero—and so, for that matter, was an eleven-year-old boy named Marco Fennerty, Junior.

The story made pleasant and exciting reading. It was

nice, Marco thought, to be famous when you're young enough to enjoy it. (Tiger, he guessed, wouldn't much care either way.)

But what about Tiger? The story just said he had been given "temporary refuge" at the zoo, which was all the reporter knew last night. The only way to be sure was to go to the zoo when it opened at nine o'clock.

Marco delivered his papers, then went to seven-fifteen mass at St. Louis Cathedral. He gave thanks that Tiger had not been shot dead on the streets and prayed that he was still safe, a permanent guest of the zoo.

When Marco got home from church, his father was waiting for him. Sergeant Fennerty was actually taking his day off. He was still in uniform and had a sack of hamburgers he had picked up on his way home from the police station. They sure beat oatmeal.

After breakfast, Marco and his father took the St. Charles streetcar to Audubon Park. The park was beautiful, with the morning sunlight slanting through the oaks and flashing on the leaves. It was cool, and the air smelled clean and green.

Early as it was, men were already washing their cars under the trees. Men in loud sports shirts and women in bright dresses were laying out picnic lunches on the grass. Their children were playing badminton and yelling at each other when one missed a shot. On the flat green lagoon a man with his sleeves rolled up was rowing a boat. He kept muttering to himself as the oars kept jumping out of the oarlocks. He had Marco's full sympathy. Streams of men, women, and children were moving through the park.

Marco and his father walked along the bridle path, following the route the boy and the tiger had taken last night. Marco showed his father Tiger's paw prints in the soft brown earth. Marco was proud to be with his father in his police-man's uniform and proud of his limp from the .45-caliber bullet wound, received in the line of duty. Obviously his father was also proud to be with Marco.

"You know, this is fun," Sergeant Fennerty remarked. "We'll have to do this every Sunday."

A big crowd was already outside the zoo. The gates were just opening.

Quickly, Marco led the way past the monkey cages—he liked monkeys (who didn't?)—but he had no time for them now. Nor for the bears. Nor for the lions. Nor for the ele-phants.

In the first cage, a tiger gazed out at him and yawned. It wasn't Tiger. Neither was the other tiger with him. In the next cage, a tiger was rubbing himself against the bars and fussing. A tiger in the corner raised up and fussed about all the fussing. In the third cage, two tigers were pacing up and down together, matching each other step for step. They stopped and looked out at Marco as if he were their Sunday dinner.

At the bottom of the fourth cage was a sign that said "Norah Sue, Royal Bengal Tiger (*Felis tigris*)." Norah Sue was lying on her back, taking the morning sun on her white belly. She seemed relaxed and happy. She twisted her head around to look at Marco and winked, or blinked, a naughty eye.

Her fangs and claws were frightening to see. She was alone in the cage.

"Oh, no!" Marco turned to his father, who squeezed his shoulder hard. The crowd pressed them against the railing.

"Hey!" someone yelled. "What's the big idea? That's not Tiger!"

The crowd began to stamp, shouting, "We want Tiger! We want *Ti-ger!*"

Marco felt ill. His father was gazing down at him sadly, still squeezing his shoulder. The boy kept staring at Norah Sue's terrible weapons, remembering what the zoo attendant had told him last night. "Norah Sue like to tear them poor tigers to shreds . . ."

"Hey, look!" someone shouted.

Into the cage through the door of the back room, where he had gone to groom himself perhaps or maybe just to think things over, came a tiger who walked with his right front paw in the air. The people cheered, but the tiger paid no attention to them. His big golden eyes were centered on his little friend.

"Hello, Tiger," Marco said softly.

"Ho!" said Tiger.

JOHN FOSTER

was born in Chicago and grew up in Oak Park, Illinois, the son of a lawyer and one of five children. During World War II he served as a Navy pharmacist's mate with the Second Marine Division in the Pacific.

Briefly, he attended the University of Wisconsin, in Madison. Later, he took a bachelor's degree from Florida Southern College, at Lakeland, and attended graduate school at the University of Florida, in Gainesville. He has worked on newspapers in Lakeland, Wilmington, North Carolina, and New Orleans, Louisiana. He is presently editor of the weekend magazine of the *Suffolk Sun*, a Long Island newspaper.

John Foster's first fiction book for children is *Marco and the Tiger*. He has had two biographies for young readers published, as well as an adult novel, brought out in the United States and Great Britain. He has written short stories and articles for national magazines in the United States, Canada, Great Britain, and the Netherlands.

When not working, John Foster likes to play badminton, swim, row, and go on long walks with his dog, George. He lives with his wife, Dusty, and two young children, Norah and John Junior, in Huntington, Long Island, New York. An older daughter, Carol, lives in New York City.